# Half Dollar Rebel:

## Annals of Hard-Boiled Determination and Dogged Misanthropy

By James R. Parkinson

ISBN: 9780985316846

# Table of Contents

## Swollen, Warped Idealism

The barista crossed me, and she had to pay. I'd outlined my revenge-plot options here on the serviette. I might manipulate the manager into firing her, but she was an affable hipster chick and he was a frumpy, tucked-in beta male almost certainly in love with her. Any complaint I made might simply provide him with leverage to make another sideways advance. I'd rather just pull the fire alarm and stick my foot out. Or whip the shaker of powdered sugar at her face. Disproportionate reactions; all she did was ask how my day was going "so far." What the hell was that supposed to mean? Her words didn't cast even a shadow of sincerity. Answering with specifics and qualifying descriptors would be seen as an overshare, despite being a literal response. She wanted a stock answer to her stock question, something I didn't keep on file. I'd instead answered, "Why don't you just steam my latte, Punky Brewster, and we'll keep the questions on ice?" I thought I was being honest and direct, but the conversation deteriorated from there. Time to cash out. I hadn't come in here to start a cold war with an airhead.

One last cup of Seattle coffee before I jetted. I left town with a knife in my teeth. It was time to go—anywhere—so I stuffed the everything-left into my Chevy Malibu at 4 a.m. and set a course for New York City. First stop would be my cousin's house in Inkom, Idaho. ETA: dusk. The Emerald City was a gift and a dream, five years of figuring it out and forging myself into the spit-and-grit Everyman Warrior, but the money dried up and the Pacific Northwest perma-drizzle swelled and warped my idealism. In a town where everyone was polite but no one was kind, I got sick of the bullshit. Seattle maintains a fog of civility and forced humanism that masks friend from foe, but if you squint hard enough and listen for sarcasm, you can pick up subtle differences. The time to leave had ticked over.

The LCD read 5:57 p.m. as I dropped out of warp and pulled into Jon's driveway. The last time I saw him we were subhuman pre-adolescents, breaking into grandpa's gun rack and sneaking cookies from the jar. Fifteen years of circling the sun with the plates shifting beneath our feet metamorphosed us both entirely: Jon shot up seven feet in height and I lost all meaningful hair from my scalp. But even over the chasm of time, we lost no synergy, picking up not quite where we left off, but rather where we should have. My knock on the door was answered with a hug and an icy Corona. The rules of the house were simple, Jon explained. Help myself to anything in the fridge, leave the toilet seat up at all times, and don't walk outside without a piece. "This is a dangerous neighborhood," he mumbled, expressionless.

"Gangs?"

"No, mountain lions."

"Good to know."

Backlogged at least a decade by lost time, we railed through a thirty rack of Coors Light in a marathon session. Thin blood and a nostalgia high led to questionable decision-making. "Jamie, I've got an idea. Let's grab some beers, jump in the truck and go run the dog." Jon's youthful Labrador retriever, Jake, boasted fathomless energy levels far surpassing those normally depleted by regular walks. He ran full bore up the mountainside as we gave chase in Jon's F-150 truck, drunk as fuck but distantly removed from pedestrians or anything else worth hitting. "He's been eating that Rachael Ray puppy chow. He's gonna shit everywhere. It's gonna be awesome!" Jon's fecalphiliac reveries merged premonition into reality. Jake's shits were truly omnipresent, often mid-stride.

Jake, Jon and I returned to the bonfire with voided bowels and a fresh sixer. Out of wood, we started burning garbage. Unrecycled boxes of Mountain Dew, Budweiser, fun-size chips, Honey Smacks et. al. were sacrificed to the heavens. When our unsettled surface thoughts cooked off with the rest of the embers, our conversation sunk a little deeper. Jon started asking questions he would never dare under the sobering light of day. "Jamie, why are you *moving*? You seem like such a badass in Seattle, with comedy and everything." I stared out into the middle distance, avoiding the subject I most desperately wanted to breach.

In Seattle I failed every career I could lay my hands on. Politics, hospitality, real estate, non-profit do-goodery, and yes, stand-up-go-fuck-yourself comedy. I ran the gamut, piloting the alternative scene's top showcase, The Laff Hole, emceeing every comedy club in the city on a regular basis, bullying newbies at open mics, sucking up to headliners on the road, performing in national festivals like Bridgetown and Bumbershoot, but always falling short of being able to make a living doing anything other than crawling back to the regular work force, unable to smash my own personal glass ceiling.

Jon is family, so he got the full story, down to the dregs. He heard the confessions, how my ego flew well ahead of my progress, rendering my talent irrelevant. He dutifully listened, nodding pensively and trying—mostly effectively—to empathize with what the experience must have been like. I told him about the endless open mics, the unattended bar shows, and the euphoric nights where real fans showed up for real comedy. That's the dragon you chase, the "some of the people" that I can please all of the time. Young, educated, sarcastic, partially cunty, irreverant, and cheap, cheap, cheap. I can't make a living performing for that crowd. Not yet anyway, so the only choice is to charm the *hoi polloi* on the road, or quit entirely. That, or get the fuck out of Seattle. "Okay, shit dude, I get it," he offered. "You think New York will be any different?" I had no answer to that, but change has always done me good before.

We boozed heavily all week, off-roading in the hills and taking target practice at piles of garbage. A press for time was my excuse, but leaving was an act of self-preservation. In truth, I had time to spare and used it. I've driven across the country before, but I always shot straight. On this trip I savored a little bit of everything. Instead of the Dakotas I chose to snake my way south, pulling over to gasp and shudder at the terrible beauty of Colorado's famed Flaming Gorge, a staggering scar of rock and earth colorfully layered with bands of geological history, orange and red and magnificent. I cut back north to Chicago, drowning myself in whiskey and Blues and having the wisdom to know the difference.

To leg out the journey I made an ill-advised, do or die, 13-hour sprint from Chicago to Queens County, NY. Residual alcohol seeping from every pore, I pushed on against my better judgment. Night fell by the time I reached Pennsylvania, and the drive changed from a long, quiet cruise to a death-defying scramble not to kill deer. I don't particularly cherish the wonder of wildlife, but a pair of antlers can really rip the shit out of your radiator grill. Near midnight the George Washington Bridge yawned into view, swallowing me into my new home of Astoria. It's a funny little burb 20 minutes out of Manhattan on the N line, mostly populated by Greeks and dislocated hipsters. I don't know who I trust less: a Greek who chooses New York winter over the white-sand beaches of Mykonos, or a between-jobs graphic designer bartending on the side, scamming the unemployment system.

My journey behind me, exhaustion claimed a photo finish to hunger. On wobbly feet I hobbled to the Neptune Diner, a magnificent beast of a restaurant by the elevated train. The facade was glimmering chrome, bannered with an ancient sign boasting, "Best Diner in New York: 1992." Only Pabst's Blue-Ribbon victory could rival this proclamation for age and irrelevance. I sat down, shoveled home a pile of eggs and toast, handed my Alaska Airlines Visa to the server and exhaled. I was home. A minute later, the waiter returned. "I'm sorry, sir. Do you have another card? This one was declined."

That was the hand I was dealt: low, unpaired and offsuit. It was time to roll up my sleeves, dig my heels into the soil and start bluffing like a madman.

## 2

## Torque Therapy

There was a car fire under the elevated subway platform. My stop hangs over Hoyt Avenue—onramp to the Triborough—and the walkway was choking on metallic smoke. Down on the street some poor bastard had kissed the guard rail longways, his Audi now gurgling a death rattle on the shoulder, screaming flames at the sky. A gaggle of rubbernecked civilians perched on the edge, chirping at each other, pecking on their iPhones, dialing 911 and snapping home video. One brave fool made a hero's effort, ditching his van to see if anyone was pinned inside. From where I stood, the driver's seat looked empty minus a spent airbag. Our hero saw the same nothing and split. If anyone was still in the car, they were butterflied and cooked through anyway.

That's kind of how it goes around here. Point A to B is a trip-mined obstacle course, littered with bumper to bumper stress heads. It's no good; you burn too much oil driving that hot. I did. I broke down entirely, even made a move to talk to a therapist about it. Then I had to fire him for being a pussy.

Acute rage and chronic anxiety; he had his work cut out for him. "Hi Doc, hope you like a project," I offered in greeting. He hated my calling him "Doc," something about having completed no such level of education. Mind wide open, I'd walked into his office, a room desperate to be comfortable. There was a shag sofa, smuggled in from the Seventies. An earthy-toned rug warmed the floor around paint-by-numbers psychology bookshelves. Our therapy largely consisted of personifying my anxieties into an avatar that I could isolate and mollify.

"James, I want you to imagine this person who is assigned to protect you. I want you to imagine who he is and what he looks like, and I want you to thank him for all he has done for you."

I imagined him as a high-school gym teacher. He had a moustache, powder-blue polo, a whistle and completed the look with a clipboard to-do list. You could tell right away he was a dick.

"I tried to thank him, Doc, but he won't talk to me."

Doc was pissed, but I wasn't kidding.

"Listen, Doc..."

"Please don't call me 'Doc.'"

"I made an accurate avatar, the anxiety cop who governs my decision-making and protects me from myself. He had shit to do; what do you want?"

Doc was upset, kind of a whiner, and I didn't really explore other options. I cut him a kiss-off check and bolted.

I wasn't supposed to do that. My folks had lobbied hard for me to see the pony-tailed bastard, and now I had to cobble together an explanation that wouldn't sound like impulsive quitting. I had an hour on the train to think about it. When I resurfaced in Queens, Andy had an answer for me, a tantrum of vibration and color. Andy, he's my cell phone, an HTC Android Badass with 512 MB of RAM, flip-out keyboard, and a hard drive large enough to house every novel, song, screenplay or dessert critique ever written by every man or babe-man who ever lived. He rides shotgun and serves a wide variety of critical functions: managing my finances, tracking appointments and screening phone calls from business contacts and jilted women. This time he red-flagged a text from Bruner: "Come to the stoop." Bruner is my neighbor, and the concrete steps ascending to his front door are a second living room to both of us.

He was buried in his own cell when I rolled up, a Budweiser tallboy sweating in his free hand and a cigarette burning idly at the end of his lips. He's a 35-year-old punk-rock survivor with two faces, one respectable. By day he is a fire inspector with the FDNY, tapping on pipes and shining a flashlight into dark spaces, making sure the architectural bones of this city are ready when the sparks start to fly. At night he is a fledgling stand-up comedian, telling bad jokes about the plight of man so that we might laugh over the ripe corpse of a dead world. He also draws robots.

I told him about the therapy breakup. "You need to buy a bike," he said between sips, a clear and willful violation of New York City's open container laws. "Get out of your head and start rolling. The city will feel smaller, and you'll feel better." As a general rule, I don't let anyone talk me into doing anything, ever. I don't order appetizers, I refuse upgrades to first class, and my prostate can go check itself for all I care. But this was too promising to pass up, and having eliminated therapy with a line-item veto, the expense was negligible. I capitulated only once Bruner agreed to accept the purchase as my idea. His spawn would have to scribble some lesser achievement on his tombstone.

Once I've made a decision, nothing short of a seismic calamity can stay the execution. I needed a bike, and according to Bruner, I needed to name it. Again, my idea. So I set Andy to work, Googling a local non-corporate bicycle shop, something free of mob ties and union affiliation. I settled on a Trek 10-speed hybrid road bike with a Kryptonite Evolution Series U-lock and flex cable. I named her "My Therapist," after the sad schmuck who tried to shrink me with his social-work degree. This summer I would be processing my anxiety through the whirling maelstrom of my bicycle's drive train: torque therapy.

## 3

## Paying Off the Midnight Waffles

This morning I confronted an officer of the
United States Postal Service. I spotted him a block
away, casing the neighborhood one house at a
time in a crisscross pattern. He stopped at *every*
door. Who was this man? What was his angle?
When he approached, I was ready for him. I kept
my eyes sealed to the peephole. My right hand
rested on the doorknob, my left held a gleaming
tack-hammer. Nobody but nobody approaches the
threshold of my domicile, not without a bag of lo
mein noodles. One step up towards the door and I
was on him, staring him down the curb and into a
puddle. "Identify yourself! Are you alone? Declare
your purpose! Are you an operative of the
government?"

The coward feigned ignorance, leaving his
earbuds in and side-stepping my interrogation. He
jammed a bundle of credit-card offers into my
hands and split. Discover, MasterCard, Citibank;
they all want a taste. The buzzards are circling

because they can smell my alpha-male credit. That's why I'm a mark. I run a high balance but never miss a payment. It's a blood sport. I never cared much for penny slots or gentleman's bets, so forgive me for quoting Lady Gaga: "Russian Roulette ain't the same without a gun." There has to be skin in the game or I won't play. I also won't be applying for any new credit cards, as I am currently engaged in all-out warfare with the bastards at Visa. They hosed me into a rotten deal years ago, tempting me into a life debt with the promise of free Alaska Airlines miles. "Free" is a four-letter word that only rings true if you can't put a dollar sign on a pound of your own flesh.

I shredded the envelopes and torched the scrappings in an iron pot. I was sweeping the ashes into a bucket of bleach when Andy squawked. Bruner again, reminding me of the show tonight. He and his roommates produce and perform on these do-it-yourself comedy shows in nontraditional locations around Queens and Brooklyn. Last time they scribbled arrows on the sidewalk and performed in a boxing ring in Dumbo, trading quips instead of haymakers. For tonight, his manager had rented the rock-star suite of a hotel in Long Island City. Admission was $20, all you can drink. I wanted to go, but I had to be up early.

I declined the invitation with great regret. I was missing too many of these. Life swirled drainward. Andy's alarm systems were set daily for 4 a.m. He dutifully woke me up every morning, and I habitually thanked him by not pulverizing him against the radiator. I had to be up and cycling over the Queensboro Bridge by sunup or else the guests missed out on their eggs benedicts. That's what I did, worked room service at a five-star luxury hotel in Midtown. My job consisted of delivering omelets and dark-roast coffee to celebrities and dot-com survivor stories. Divulging the guests' identities was strictly prohibited. In fact, it was Service Standard #14 of our zeitgeist: "Be respectful of our guest's personal time and privacy, delivering service that does not interrupt or interfere with our guest's activities. Never approach a guest to request a favor, such as an autograph." I collected them anyway, via Andy snapping a small grainy photograph of their signed room-service slips in case I ever need to forge a high-powered

17

signature in a sensitive situation. You never know...but I do.

It wasn't a job, it was a prison sentence. I loathed the task of rushing breakfast to uppercrust elites with bulletproof bank accounts and Centurion Amex cards made out of anodized titanium. Alas, that was the mission. The hotel was an infant, barely one year old and deathly terrified of an old enemy: unionization. In an effort to thwart organized labor we all made money well over our position, including magical benefits like vacation pay, sick pay and health and dental insurance. I even got an eight-hour freebie just for my birthday rolling past on the calendar. It was the fourteenth job I'd held in two years of living in New York City, and at this point it was a joyless chore, merely a means to an end.

The punishment was beyond harsh. My debt was the bastard child of carelessness and life lived in the moment. I should have been more careful, taken steps to ensure more money came in than went out. Prescient of consequence, I did the wrong thing anyway. Life felt liquid, impossible to grasp and ever-evaporating into the ether. Responsibility could wait, so I put it on the shelf to deal with at a better time that never came. Digging out was going to take some doing. I had to triage the whole situation and prioritize monotony and diligence over gut instinct and spontaneity. Every balance transfer was a minor victory, followed by a cash-poor hangover. The euphoria remained short-lived when I was paying interest on rounds of drinks and midnight waffles vomited against the side of a Wells Fargo four years ago. There was plenty of uphill before me, but I was no Sisyphus. I was about to shot put that financial boulder clear across the cosmos, nothing but net.

## 4

## Low and Slow/Occupy Chili

This morning I set out to reinvent the concept of chili.

I ventured into the grocery store without a map. Recipes are for cowards. Cooking is an act of violent creation. I'm not selling square hamburgers and meals that deliver "happiness" to children in the form of congealed fat and a colorful plastic choking hazard. When I cook, I offer nothing but a promise that whatever you taste, it will be for the first time.

My game plan didn't fit the accepted definition of "chili," but I don't give a particular shit about the gutless opinions of Food Network peons. I started with a traditional base of diced tomatoes, tomato paste, kidney beans, white beans, garlic cloves, a bit of cumin and lots of onion. I have respect for the onion, a vicious, nasty species, king of the vegetable kingdom. Onions fight back against the dicing blade, releasing airborne countermeasures that irritate the tear ducts and send rookie knife-handlers running for the eyewash station. Two-hundred-pound weight advantage, standing in my own house, wielding a stainless-steel Japanese blade, and I'm the one crying. Veggies in the pot, I unpacked the meat.

I cubed two large rib-eye steaks, rolled a couple dozen ground pork balls and diced up half a pack of applewood smoked bacon, all free range. We conquered the food chain long ago, so I have no qualms about eating meat. I do, however, insist any animal that dies at my hand be permitted to spend its life grazing freely under God's sky. There is nothing so craven as the consumption of tortured meat. The final touch was half a can of chipotle chilies, a spicy little catalyst designed to make the whole thing light up like a barge fire. I flipped the Crock on low as Andy the Android began to sing from within my pocket. It was Bruner calling, eager to go on a long bike ride one last time before summer withered. There was plenty of time; chili takes about eight hours cooking low and slow to transmogrify from a mob of independent, mercenary ingredients into a cohesive movement of single-purposed flavor. I set Andy's alarm to chirp at 4 p.m., grabbed My Therapist and set out.

When I rolled up to Bruner's stoop he was hunched over his ride, which was wheels-up for maintenance. His left hand held an oily rag and a bottle of degreaser. His right hand furiously scrubbed grime and dirt from his bicycle chain with his ex-girlfriend's pink Oral-B Contour Clean Indicator. I leaned My Therapist against the fence and bought deli coffee across the street while Bruner tightened everything with Allen wrenches and filled our tires with compressed air. We shot the shit, talked about pussy for a half minute and set out for Zuccotti Park, shredding pavement on our way to the Occupy Wall Street protests.

The propaganda-cable cabal had cut some self-interested footage of the event; we wanted to see for ourselves what these characters were up to. You could hear them before you saw them, on account of the filibustering 24-hour drum circle. I came for the chimes of freedom, but these dudes were meth-addled percussion addicts. We locked our bikes to a barrier fence and cut through the park past aging hippies, scrubby punk-rock anarchists, vulturous photographers and media operatives, stoic police officers and borderline personalities looking for a place to enjoy their manic phase. The occupants of the park had one vaguely unifying descriptor: poor and pissed. Beyond that they were a muddled collection of unkempt riffraff. Those with a clear, coherent message and an eternally valid point of view on socioeconomic justice were flanked at all sides by vapid bongo players and willfully unemployed miscreants falling over themselves to undermine their own movement.

The Williamsburg Bridge shuffled beneath our homeward wheels. Less than a mile from the epicenter of Mankind's latest stab at a fair shake for as many people as possible, and I was already thinking about the banal minutia of my day-to-day: how I had to be up early tomorrow and needed to get to bed before 9, that laundry day was approaching, how to best avoid my boss, how I needed to transfer money into my savings account, and that I just stood in the heart of change and felt nothing.

It's too bad. There was a lot of promise, with mirror protests popping up in every major city, including tiny satellite gatherings in small towns across the country. The reach of this movement extended across the ocean, drawing crowds from San Francisco to London. I heard they even got the pigs to use tear gas in Rome. Funny thing about tear gas: it's a coward's weapon designed for peaceful targets with valid, defensible points of view. I hoped this feeble alliance held its ground. I run too hot for this shit. If I had my way, I'd set up a guillotine to shorten a few FOX News assholes and hedgefund managers at the neck, French Revolution style. But we don't live in that world anymore. Ghandi set the gold standard. These kids needed to keep doing whatever they are doing, applying pressure and heat, low and slow until something gives.

Bruner and I parted ways wordlessly at the corner. I jangled my keys through both apartment doors and shouldered My Therapist up the stairs and into the kitchen. Andy startled chortling like a madman. Eight hours of change and the chili was done. Beaded with moisture, the Crock Pot cover shackled back a pocket of steam.

The dark surface chattered with bubbles. I sniffed the air point-blank: sweet, smoky bouquet of tomato, thick and meaty, latent heat. The back of my throat squared for a fight. I test drove with a wooden spoon, stirring against resistance, loading up with chunks of perfectly stewed beef and pork, sporadic vegetables and cluttered beanery. Pausing to let it cool, eyes closed and mind open, I chewed slowly, savoring the taste and texture. Revolution.

## 5

## New York City Fadeout

My periodontist asked me to fuck his daughter. It was during surgery, a fairly minor procedure. He stuck me with a six-inch dagger of Novocaine and hacked into my gum line to chisel out 30 years of horrific rot. Wiping bloody chunks of flesh onto my lobster bib, he jammed two fingers into my cheek and commenced the interrogation. How old was I? Where did I live? What did I do for a living? "I want you to call my daughter. She broke up with her boyfriend a month ago, and she's hot."

He dangled the suction wand on my lip like a cocktail garnish, ducking out to grab his loinsfruit's headshot and a prescription slip with her name and number. The headshot was a tragic mess, completely unacceptable. I might have called if her name was Vicodin and her number 1-800-4-Refills. Sensing my disinterest, Doc stood up, taken aback. Bastard had no right to conjure tension; I was the one with a hemorrhaging jaw.

So I stared him down, pulling my lip into a "Fuck you" snarl, straining through the local anesthetic and nitrus fog until he yielded, "Well, you're not obligated or anything." Goddamn right. I then noticed he was wearing roller skates, a startling accessory for a licensed medical professional on the Upper East Side. Sir, are you out of your mind? I'm not putting my dick anywhere near those genes.

That's love in the City. I had a date lined up a while back, and an hour before meeting the female in question I received "James honey I'm drunk, I don't want you to meet me like this." Andy dictated the text message for me, received from a knockout poptart I met via OkCupid, a dating site for bargain hunters, sexual predators and those of us who know that a life well-lived is going to cost some skin. I'd squared up and created my profile: a detailed personal manifesto, line by line prerequisites for interested applicants and my complete medical history including monthly weigh-ins, cholesterol levels and magnetic resonance imagery. Also a shirtless photo of myself holding a puppy by the ocean.

I began composing a reply, something along the lines of a raincheck, when she followed up with, "if you are persistent, however, i will be on stone street for another hour or so." Game on. I stepped into some jeans, splashed my throat with tequila and hit the throttle. I found Keisha on the cobblestones. She was arresting; a Perfect 10 with fuck-me heels and a black dress, onyx eyes and a smoke trail. My spine bolted straight and the neurons in my brain flared like the broadside of a battleship. Here was a live one, and none too soon. It had been a thin season on an ocean that was habitually over-fished.

And now there was Keisha, burning through the fog, ferocious and aggressive. She dragooned me to her lair, a dark, anonymous Irish bar, a temple of alcohol and escapism. Her commands came hot and fast. "James, darling, I'm going to order water and then I'm going to the ladies room. It's a cover; I need to steal this pint glass. Do you understand me? Now order something strong and drink it." Someone with fangs, finally. A worthy adversary.

In her absence Andy shrieked out a

warning. Checking into Foursquare, he noted that Keisha was the "Mayor" of the bar, a critical red flag whipping at the parapet. Too late, she was on me, one leg hooked on my stool, shoved between mine. We locked eyes and cut past the life-story bullshit, whispering only truths about sex and drugs, her fingers tracing my wrist. Everything was hurtling along at a steady clip until she brought up her pug. It was a ridiculous aside, insane and irrelevant. I couldn't endure this diversion. It threatened every skillet on the stove. So to shut her up, I kissed her full-on under the glow of a Heineken sign. Her lip gloss was a peculiar strain of venom; she pressed in firm and writhed on her stool like a leopard on a branch. Somehow, too drunk for mistakes, we left everything dangling on the edge of a cliff. I walked her across the street and safely to her door; she clutched me by the collar, demanding promises about "doing this again" before vanishing into her building. I shuttled home to Astoria on the N train.

And just like that, it was over. She shot me with my own bullet, a little trick called the New York City Fadeout. In a city of eight million people, everyone chasing stars and scrambling for cash, it was perfectly legitimate to fill your schedule until a love interest simply gave up and faded away. That's the game out here. Love is a beast, and the species' leading cause of death is exposure. When you realized someone isn't The One, you put them on the fade. It really was for the best. I was a Midtown service-industry professional, she a Financial District dollar-chasing bitch with an unhealthy attachment to an inbred glamour pet. I could only imagine what I'd have said to her the first time she snapped at me for wearing a hoodie to dinner or leaving a dish in the sink.

There is great serenity in singularity, a promise for the unknown, the sunrise of possibility glazing the next horizon. I just had to go get it.

## 6

## Keep Your Trigger Moving

The enemy approached. I could hear them squeaking against each other. Ten thousand helium balloons, maybe more. A bloody shitstorm of fire-retardant latex and iron-plated polychloroprene, self-propelled and broiling into an unstoppable horde just behind the horizon of the battle track. Let them come. Surveying the field, I saw that my army of monkeys was ready. The front line was a wedge formation of dart-chuckers flanked by glue-launchers to slow the enemy advance. My boomerang specialists were dug in at the midpoint just past the second bend, perfect positioning to arc their glaives along the approach strip for maximum kill potential. I had heavy artillery—and plenty of it—holding the rear, long-range spigot mortar units armed with 320 millimeter high-explosive-tipped warheads and white phosphorous incendiary payload. A bloody sun rose, leaving streaks across the sky. Let's get Biblical.

Free internet gaming: it ain't living, but such fare as Bloons Tower Defense 4 kept the brainpan functioning at a high level while I was clawing my way out of debt, trying not to go mad. Resources were thin. Year one was the real mud fight. I maxed out the Visa right away and stepped into the NYC octagon with a pronounced limp. The job hunt launched immediately, roaring out of the subway the following afternoon with a fistful of resumes.

I strode first into a place called Butler's. I found out later the place was named for *Gone with the Wind*'s Rhett Butler, which explained such slavery/racism-themed menu items as "The Plantation Burger." Apparently one of the servers begged "Mammy's Fried Chicken" not be included; a minor victory.

The owner, a hulking British transplant, was lurking at the front door. He glanced at my resume (and, I suspect, the color of my white skin) and immediately dragged me further inside for an interview. I was hired, but it didn't last. The place was a disaster. Broken espresso machine, lousy food, no clientele to speak of minus a

handful of drunks and irregular regulars
(including inimitable dragon-bitch Nancy Grace).
Cash came in a trickle, and the dam broke when I
witnessed the owner dragging a co-worker across
the floor by his collar for asking a customer if
they'd like whipped cream on their Irish coffee. If
he'd tried that on me he'd have heard his wrist
bones snap prior to kissing the floor.

A real and accurate Yelp.com review:

*Ever walk into a bar and get the sense
that the entire 'staff' and all the 'patrons' had only
just moments before committed a grisly murder
and you're the first one to walk into the bar as
they collectively struggle to keep a straight face?
"EVERYONE BE COOL! BE COOL!" they might
have just been heard to scream before we walked
into Midtown East's very own Butler's.*

*"You guys gonna order food?" The goon
bartender asked while straightening his tie, as if
to say, 'There's nothing to see here.' I'd go back to
Butler's, but I'm afraid that since they've seen my
face, I'm now some sort of accomplice. Having
said all that, I guess the sweet potato fries were
pretty good.*

The key to victory in trench warfare is to keep your head down and trigger moving. You have to manage resources and maintain pressure. A faceless enemy like this wasn't vulnerable to a single killstroke; no, the balloons keep coming. That's what they do. For every war ape I positioned on the ridgeline, the enemy countered with a thousand fluttering party weapons, snaking relentlessly up the slope and past my companions, exhausted and buried in their own spent shell casings.

I lined up a gig before leaving Butler's, another restaurant in another neighborhood. It was their grand opening, a cute little boutique spot stretching its legs for the first time. I was to be the ace of their staff. One job going out, a new one coming in, and my car was listed on Craigslist for $3000. The whole situation had a pulse. I wasn't beaten yet—not by a long shot—and when I looked down at my hands, I saw fists.

## 7

## Goodbye, My Love

You were a bolt of lightning. For a time I held you in my fist, crackling around my knuckles, snapping at my belt buckle with your forked tongue, vibrating the fillings in my teeth, fusing the change in my pockets. But I let you go, and with you went a seared chunk of myself. Now you are forever lost. The stars are banished from the sky; if I had the strength to gaze above, there would be nothing but an errant jetliner. The faucets pour sand, fixtures cast more shadow than light, fresh produce turns to chalk in my mouth.

My darling, though we had driven through so much together, I failed you. Our collective miles traced the seam of the ocean, the hem of the mountains, melted into sunsets together. We visited the ghettos of hell and came home with souvenirs. It was all my fault; was I who gave up on you. We may have run out of road, but there was gas left in the tank—I know there was!—I could hear you purring until I disengaged the key and threw you in park forever.

I'll never forget you, nor the day we met. I was a hotshot intern in professional baseball and you were a silver blade, unsheathed and gleaming brazenly in the gridlocked masses of lesser, haggard rivals. We drove together to Modesto, high on petrol, "Idiot Wind" blowing from the speakers. We had swagger, potential, determination and little else. We didn't need it, and we didn't care. We were together. You followed me to Seattle when I asked you to, then sat in the rain waiting for lights to bleed from red to green. For five years we made it work, and for most of it we didn't even have to try. It was our journey. We were a Fellowship of two.

You followed me further to New York. The trip itself was a song; you carried me as you always have. Six cylinders humming along, breathing the miles, oblivious to the uncertainty of the future even as clouds gathered. But New York couldn't work; wouldn't work. Too many people and too few streets. There was nowhere for you to park, and I just didn't need you anymore.

Not like before.

Can you ever forgive me? I now have the train, a 24-hour operation with comprehensive service and consistent reliability. No insurance, no gas, no DUIs. Surely you understand; surely you remember that close call when we faced fate together and nearly lost everything.

We were driving home from that show in September. I was the comedian, the thoughtless one, following the officer's flashlight with my eyes, touching my nose with my finger, trying to walk a straight line, fumbling the alphabet in reverse. You idled nervously on the shoulder while I kissed the breathalyzer. I blew zeroes and you blew an opaque brown cloud from the muffler. The first sign of trouble.

I couldn't hold on, even though I wanted to. The restaurant fired me; didn't even give me a reason. I loved that place, a quaint neighborhood spot with great food, and the guests loved me in return. But it was the wrong fit. Management even offered to recommend me somewhere else, but it didn't ease the pain, and it certainly didn't cover the rent. I needed the money, and you were a $4,000 car. Everyone said so but the buyers. They saw your scars, where I scraped the dumpster and some asshole clipped us at McDonald's. They saw your breath rasping out of the exhaust pipe. Worst of all, they saw the service light when I turned your key. I refused to believe it when they said you were dying inside. I denied it. I defied it. "This is a great car!" I would thunder. "I just drove her across the country with no problems!" They didn't care. Mechanics and risk-averse shoppers don't look at engines and see heart. They didn't know how you hugged the road on tight curves, or how you started right up even when frost had your throat in its icy grip. They don't know what I knew about you. They couldn't love you like I did, like I still do. A second opinion, and a third, and a fourth, and I sold you out for half your Blue Book value. A couple months' rent and a few trips to the deli. I fucked up, and I can never get you back.

I got a new job selling steaks in Midtown soon enough after the firing. (It was to be the first of many.) I'm still riding the train, but I miss you dearly. The streets are lined with strangers. Some

Jeep asshole keeps parking in your spot. I hope you are well, that your tires are full, that your new owner knows not to ride the brakes and to keep you several car lengths behind the vehicle in front of you. I hope your airbags are undeployed and your CD player is functioning properly and Bieber-free. Maybe I will see you again someday, idling at a stop sign or sipping gas at the Sunoco. And if I don't see you on the roads, I'll remember you in those passing moments, when the clock strikes Ten and Two, and any time when I have somewhere to be and no one to take me there. Goodbye, my love.

# 8

## Fallacy Frosting and the Blood Hunt

Why was I awake? Confronted directly, the darkness answered back with more darkness. It was 2 o'clock in the morning and I had stumbled into consciousness for no detectable reason or purpose. I didn't have to be up yet, and Andy the Android was silent. If it were wake-up time he'd have been vibrating all over the desk and singing his alarm for me, whining for attention like a puppy with a full bladder. Instead he lay silently on his back, snoring softly through a green charge-indicator light, suckling the USB cable from my MacBook.

Confounded, I listened carefully for the crackle of gunfire. My roommate wakes me up sometimes in the middle of a firefight, trading hot lead with South American drug cartels on the Xbox in the next room. Tonight there was no sound, and yet I lay awake, pissed. I needed to be asleep. I needed to hit something.

This was hell week, eight straight workdays in the hotel. It's a scheduling anomaly, the bi-product of honoring co-workers' time-off requests. Ours was a 24-hour operation, open for business 100 percent of every passing moment in the year. We were constructs of brick and beams, holding up the same tower. If one of us took a vacation, someone else had to reach up and keep the roof affixed snugly to the walls. I was happy to do it...but I couldn't face those faces, goddammit, not without rest.

It wasn't so much the work itself. Boiling coffee into a pot and wheeling Eggs Benedicts into a bedroom isn't much of a calorie burner. It's the mask we had to wear; the all-day fabrication I told. Therein lay the struggle. One example: My corporate masters maintained a completely absurd prejudice against facial hair. If I would like to continue working for the company, I was required to participate in a daily ritual that raged against my lifestyle.

Every morning I stood in the bathroom for those bastards, scraping hot razors against the grain of my skin to meet an arbitrary "grooming standard" that didn't apply to such bearded legends as Jim Henson, 16th President Abraham Lincoln, Aragorn Son of Arathorn, and Eternal Savior/Jew Carpenter Jesus H. Christ of Nazareth. I suppose the residents of my hotel preferred to own slaves in a Muppet-less universe ruled by the Dark Lord Sauron, unaware of whose name to scream in vain over a stubbed toe.

That was just the frosting of the fallacy, not yet part of the cake. One guest from a major hip-hop label abandoned all street cred by throwing a fit when we brought him Tropicana instead of juice squeezed to order. Insane. Our species doesn't eat regionally anymore; we don't even know what "squeezed to order" would mean. Oranges don't grow in winter. Nothing does except kale and roots. Produce doesn't keep well, either, unless you put it in a can. Your best hope for freshness, if you aren't smuggling shipments up from Chile, is to keep crates of apples in cold storage. Desiring fresh, imported orange juice is acceptable. Demanding it betrays a childish misunderstanding of what it even is. I had to smile at these people through sinewy hatred, apologizing for unjustified reasons against my will.

So why the hell was I awake? The answer came from my skin: I was on fire. I itched everywhere, and my face was covered with welts. This was bad.

A lot can go wrong living in New York. You can lose track of your dreams; get your heart broken. You can lose your faith in God or fall on the subway tracks, barbecuing your organs on the third rail. Some folks get mugged walking home from the bar, or clipped by a cab driver distracted by his cell phone. Others get their credit card numbers "borrowed" for strange overseas purchases. You can also get bed bugs, Cimex Lectularius, a near-microscopic cunt of a species that lives in wood and feeds on human flesh. The little bastards are resistant to pesticides and can survive up to a year without eating. Getting rid of bed bugs is a simple two-step process: first you throw away all of your possessions, and then you give up. If I had bed bugs, then this New York adventure was ready to sing its death rattle.

Then I heard him, my ancient foe—a mosquito—whittling away the silence with his

43

signature whine. I had never been so happy to cross paths with a hated nemesis. Mosquitoes are real bastards to me. I grew up in New England as their own personal chain restaurant. Parky: the Cheesecake Factory of mosquito casual dining. I attract them in droves, and my skin likes to react by erupting into nasty golf-ball-sized welts. I hate mosquitoes, but at least this meant I wasn't facing bed bugs. This was good; this I could roll with. Sometimes you just need someone to kill.

Combat! Coursing with adrenaline, I assumed an attack stance, leaping to my feet on top of the bed, my body nude and pulled taught, ready to spring. I sleep naked; human skin is an organ and it needs to breathe. I flattened my hands, fingers clenched tight against each other, fashioning two lethal paddles. I was hunting a microscopic predator, but my stance was appropriate for battle with a much larger beast, something along the lines of a wyvern or a basilisk.

My walls were blank, nowhere to hide, a stark wasteland. And there he was, bold as the weather, perched just over my pillow like a fat kid vulturing the chicken-wing table at prom, drunk with blood, hiding in the open. It seemed a shame to kill him, an otherwise worthy adversary caught in a moment of anomalous weakness. Normally a stealthy predator, he was caught sleeping off a food coma on the sofa. It would be like gunning down a Nazi Stormtrooper mid-shit.

I cocked my wrist back like the hammer on a pistol, bug wings lined up in my sights. Then I paused, pangs of guilt and empathy staying my blow, the cream-and-stock base ingredients of hesitation bisque. What was he thinking? Weekend plans? Maybe how he'd house hunt for a stagnant puddle, settle down and raise a family of millions. That bastard had earned my respect. It was December, after all. He survived long past his season and somehow permeated a sealed windowsill to snack on my flesh. Who was I to halt the course of his life? Perhaps the best thing would be to grant amnesty and usher him out of the apartment?

Enraged yet pensive, enemy's head on the block, I gazed into the bedroom window, my reflection gazing back. A nude executioner, axe

45

raised, nostrils flaring as the appointed priest solemnly delivered last rites to this death-row inmate. Dead Bug Walking. There I was, strung tight, glazed with stress, swarmed with anticipation of the pending kill strike or a last-second stay of execution from the governor of my conscience. And there, in the center of my reflection's forehead, a fresh welt blossomed on a hairless scalp. He got me good. I saw red, my mouth tasted like batteries, my toes curled in rage. No. Fucking. Way. This son of a bitch sat on my face like it was a bar stool, running a tab on stolen credit, drinking heavy and tipping light.

I know how he saw me—nude, bald, pale—a hulking monster, talking food. I saw him right back, the part-time predator, a hack foe, incapable of originality or self-love, dangerous but hardly insurmountable. My hand swung free and true, flat and deadly. I slapped the wall with excessive force, hard enough to kill a dog. Because fuck him anyway, that's why. In that last moment, before his body lost dimension, before I smeared my own blood from his distended belly across the drywall, I swear to God I think he asked me to shave.

## 9

## Life is Going to Be This Way,
## Chandler Bing

Life went bad there for a bit, and had to be placed on blocks in the garage. The gas tank was always full but the oil was too thick; my brakes got sticky and the ignition turned only against its will. With elbow grease, a sharp eye and plenty of protein I'd been putting it all back together.

The road back was daunting but finite...so long as my will could bear it. It takes good, clean fuel to be a distance-running philosopher/warrior, so I cook, and I cook well.

There was a ruthless efficiency to tonight's dinner: one chicken breast and a neat pile of steamed broccoli uncorrupted by cream, butter, cheese or seasoning of any kind. I wasn't going to doll this sustenance up like a prostitute just to appease the hedonism of my taste buds. If I took their marching orders my plate would be a circus of empty carbohydrates and high-fructose escapism. They would have me lying on the ground like a fat dog, addicted to sugar and white flour, disinterested in life or love, waiting only for the fleeting respite of my next meal. In order to progress, the weakest parts of myself must be heavily mitigated for the war effort.

It was a good spread, both healthy and ethical. Free-range poultry, certified organic vegetables and a large glass of filtered water mixed with Mexican chia seeds. On the side, my horse pills: St. John's Wort, fish oil, milk thistle and a multivitamin. I was recharging after a brutal home workout. Four max-rep sets of pull-ups, sit-ups, push-ups and air squats followed by a fore-foot jog across the Triborough Bridge. On the Randall's Island side of the water there's a nice staircase perfect for metabolic training and incline sprints.

This marked the end of another good day. Anyone can have one good day; I celebrated because I'd managed to string a few of them together. I speared a flower of broccoli with my fork and chew pensively. *Friends* was coming on.

I never missed an episode, shoehorning time into my schedule for every single airing with the sense of urgency of a diabetic managing his insulin levels. It's not that I liked the show per se. I didn't. I didn't even like most of the characters. I couldn't give a cold, loveless fuck for anyone but Chandler and Monica. Ross was a risk-averse dullard with a terrific sense of entitlement and no ability to follow through for anyone but himself. Joey was a womanizing narcissist, and Phoebe desperately needed therapy for her chopped salad of psychological issues.

Worst of all was Rachel, the flat-stomached and voluptuous human void. She was a ghoul, the walking dead, a vampire, California good looks plastered over the mottled tissue beneath her skin mask, a Decepticon that transformed into a bitch. Her spectacular debut into the cultural Zeitgeist was volcanic. Men lusted over her and women championed her hairstyle as the paragon of the Nineties. The rich girl slumming it in her $4000 New York apartment, condescending to struggle but always walking the tightrope falsely, gainfully aware of the safety netting below. I can't respect a gambler placing bets with borrowed money.

So I didn't watch to keep tabs on Ross and Rachel. They should both die alone, empty husks who never learned how to see past their own reflections. I didn't watch to see Phoebe spiral further and further from mental health, and I didn't watch to see who Joey gives his HPV to next. I didn't care about Rachel's fashion career, or why they bought a chicken and a duck, and I didn't want to know about Gunther, Central Perk or Ugly Naked Guy across the street, either. I watched for Chandler Bing and Monica Geller, the only characters on the show with the capacity to feel.

Monica was a good egg, the fat girl from high school who got it together. She learned how to mix vegetables into her diet from time to time and get 20 minutes of exercise a day, a completely logical and 100 percent effective approach to losing weight. She now ran upon the food and beverage treadmill as myself, a life of endless toil in the service of Americans who can't stop eating. Then there was Chandler, my hero. My heart beat double time for this man. Known to the group and the fans as "the funny one," that's not who I saw. I saw a terribly sad soul, standing desperately against the storm, parrying blows artfully with sarcasm and cynicism, snowed in by his own shortcomings. Chandler was miscast professionally as a statistical analyst. This man was born with the soul of a writer, asphyxiated and left for dead long ago by vacant parents and compromised love. These "Friends" couldn't help him; wouldn't know where to start if they tried. No, they leaned on him, taking advantage of his empathy and his generosity, looking to him at every turn for comic relief when he needs help the most. Then there was his obvious struggle with addiction. He battled tobacco, fell in and out of love with Janice, padded around his apartment enrobed and slipper-shod, and his weight fluctuated dramatically. In season three he ballooned up maybe 30 pounds, binge eating while the girls across the hall baked him cookies and let him slip away.

This show wasn't about friendship; it was a caricature of what friendship has become. Co-dependent escapists indulging in the shallowest of their desires, ignoring the derelict engines in their own hearts as they stray from broken relationship to broken relationship. Not me, brother. I ain't going out like that. I was going to do my calisthenics, hard boil my eggs and hike onwards against all manner of resistance. Broke, indebted, overweight, undernourished and lonely, the river ran dry but its bed was gilded with faith, compounding daily, enough to carry me to whatever end so long as I remained willing to take each step under my own power.

## 10

## Every Beach Can't Be Normandy

I was carving gouges on Avenue A, separating pedestrian and vehicular traffic with grace and precision, pedaling hard and spraying gravel, when some podunk land-locked Iowa tourist prick bastard fuck stepped out of his cab, transforming the open space stretched in front of me into an impassable wall. It's called getting doored, and it's just about the worst fear a cyclist has, because it can happen at any time and there's damn near nothing you can do to prevent it. Most human beings don't exit vehicles into traffic without looking, but Mankind has an extraordinary threshold for stupidity.

I handled the accident with a certain, reckless elegance, popping off the seat like toast, spinning off the door and into the street. My forearms took the worst of the impact, suffering a few bloody brushstrokes. I didn't even leave my feet, sticking the landing and jogging a few extra steps to exhale the gravity of what could have been. Even My Therapist 10-speed was fine: no breakage, no dents, no scratches. This wasn't an accident; it was a cosmic favor. I was moving too fast, both on the street and in my life, and it was starting to degrade the fidelity of my progress and affect everything I do.

Sustainability, sustainability, sustainability. That's the key and the key and the key. Without it I was cutting asinine corners, throwing elbows in front of umpires, weaving across the highway lines and stepping on rakes all day. For disaster, just add water. My behavior had grown strange. I even found a way to sleep at work. My technique was undetectable. In the room-service office there is a POS system and two telephones with a printer under the desk. To sleep on the sly, I jammed my feet on top of the printer, wedged my knees up against the bottom of the desk and pressed my forehead flush against the cabinet above the computer. It was uncomfortable as shit and I didn't get any real rest, but I could close my eyes and shut down all the memory-hog applications that slow my brain's operating capacity. Visually I appeared to be awake, as I wasn't slumped over the desk or sprawled out with my feet up. I even passed a field test, acting startled and disoriented but quite conscious when the overnight manager walked in. I'm sure he thought my behavior odd, but that's a common conception at this point. When "Harmless Lunatic" is your modus operandi, people stop checking you for weapons.

I was well aware I should not be sleeping at work. I own a bed and needed to use it. Chalk it up to plan-design failure. I never should have volunteered for the graveyard shift; it was a critical error. The corporate masters pay 89 cents more on the hour for employees who work dusk to dawn, a moderate compensation for sacrificing a normal lifestyle. I'd fallen victim to the classic Tortoise and the Hare parable: the goal was to get healthy and pay off debt, something that can't be done by grasping for short-term gains. I slept until 3 p.m., ate eggs mid-afternoon and bid "Good Morning!" to neighbors returning home from work. That wasn't a tongue slip; I did it on purpose. Why should I alter my reality to make other people feel more comfortable?

And then I hit the door. Hard. There were

no serious injuries, but the experience was painful and scary enough to imbue me with an otherwise foreign notion: wisdom. I would need— and use— it from there on out.

The worst thing about battling debt was coping with despair, the knowledge that it is not foe but merely fog. If only it were something I could fight. To quote Arnold in *Predator*, "If it bleeds, we can kill it." Not this time. No blood and no pulse, just intangible numbers, ethereal in form, untouchable yet crushing. So I learned patience. I stopped sleeping at work. I talked to HR and confessed that the overnights were killing me. I stopped charging what I couldn't afford. I admitted that this was a marathon and not a sprint. Every beach can't be Normandy.

I was back on mornings: up at 4 a.m., skipping to the train at 5. Booze was out of my life except for special occasions where I played hockey on the Xbox. Carbs were benched, protein bats leadoff and cleanup, and the rest of the lineup was filled with greens and beans. Rest was a priority, and wouldn't you know, sanity had started poking around the tent: a warming and

welcome deja vu. I wasn't looking so far ahead
now, but keeping my eyes on the pavement
directly in front of me. And yes, still riding the
bike, meeting with My Therapist whenever
January lightens up enough for me to get in a few
miles further through my purgatorial commute.

## 11

## Man's Triumph and the
## Vengeance of Sparrows

I can usually tell if a restaurant is going to be shit right away, but this place toed the line. The specials on the white board were spelled correctly, a goddamn miracle in modern times. The Marlins on the wall were carved out of wood, a bizarre half-measure parody of the practice usually reserved for trophy space, PETA-approved. The flighty hostess sprained her brain cell puzzling over the seating map. Her mind was stalling all over the road, spinning tires and coughing exhaust, struggling to wrangle the choke point of a tourist trap while scheming a life path that might lead to fucking the busboy—clarification—that might lead to fucking the busboy again. The rest of her brainpan was occupied by an iPhone vaguely hidden under a copy of *US Weekly*, the lesser of two evils running interference for her nasty Facebook habit. It was a major victory to be sat by the window.

Water spots adorned my silverware. It's not a health issue; water spots occur because the silver isn't wiped dry after sanitizing in the Hobart machine. It's hardly poison, but why didn't they bother to clean it? Now I have doubts about their dairy. How long am I likely to be sentenced to the toilet?

My server's name was Austin. A joyless incompetent, he carried himself awkwardly, behaving as if born in borrowed skin. His voice droned artlessly over the specials, subtext screaming, "I don't want to be here! I ought to be out looking for my real face!" I went with the cioppino.

Anemic with confidence, Austin painted the linen with broth before my plate touched the table. I didn't care, not with this feast. It was fantastic. I considered announcing, "I am happy as a clam," but took a closer look at the clams in my bowl and revisited the idiom's meaning entirely. In addition to clams there were mussels, Dungeness crab, scallops and two golden wedges of toasted garlic bread. For these shellfish, life was not a comedy. They were plucked from the sea and boiled alive collectively, their bodies arranged artfully in an abattoir of saffron and tomato broth to be devoured by a superior humanoid life form. I washed them down to hell with a glass of delicately balanced Sauvignon Blanc.

Andy the Android checked me into Tides seafood restaurant on Foursquare, then asked if I would like to leave any helpful tips for the sociosphere. The restaurant was perched by the sea in Bodega Bay, California, the famous locale of Alfred Hitchcock's *The Birds*, so I warned future patrons to keep one eye on the sky lest the local wildlife take up arms. Also, try the barbecue oysters.

*The Birds* is one of my all-time favorites. The basic plot:

> Pretty face meets handsome fella in San Francisco
>
> Love story spills over into quaint sea town
>
> Millions of birds form psychic alliance, viciously attack mankind

We deserved it, too. Birds have a robust list of grievances and a comprehensive blueprint for a bloody revolution. We took the dodo first, a completely defenseless creature neither swift nor clever. We whacked them off of the planet like so many golf balls into the sea. And we didn't stop there; a different avian species seems to sputter out of existence every day. Bald eagles are in trouble, condors are almost gone, and the Passenger Pigeon KIA. There are plenty of chickens around but they exist as tortured slaves, mutated by hormones to grow at alarming rates. Their breasts and legs swell with meat so efficiently that they lose all ability to walk, and their organs begin to fail. Antibiotics keep them healthy enough to remain edible, sustaining them as they bloat into caricatures of their true species, and then it's off to the killing cones. Good night, sweet chicklings; soon we'll liquify you into delicious Clown Food McNuggets. With the exception of a few free-range cousins, a chicken sold in America never tastes free air, never feels sunshine on her wings, never learns the loving embrace of a devoted rooster. Life for her is permanent midnight, illuminated only by the screams of her sisters. We, Man, deserve to be flayed alive by suddenly prescient, vengeful sparrows.

I am grotesquely overstuffed. I shelved all principles of moderation for this meal in favor of abject gluttony. I'm on vacation, a foreign concept for me. My brain never truly allows respite. Working or not, my demons are always punched in and collecting overtime. The sole perk of self-loathing is the occasional synergy I have with said demons. They play nice when I bask in the glory of our triumph. We won, baby. We took over the planet, and thus I lean back in my chair and gaze out to sea. The bowl before me is a pile of subjugated shells. A pair of seals swims by the dock outside. Droplets of condensation glisten on the outside of my wine glass. I can't find Austin for the check; he's probably flustered by some breadstick problem or whatever. He played no role in our victory anyway.

Just outside the window two gulls perch on a life preserver and discuss gull-related concerns. I wish I could help them out; email them a PDF of Hitchcock's masterpiece. Come on, dudes, get your shit together. Man has a technological advantage, no doubt, but you have the numbers. What good are Navy Seals and stealth drones against 400 billion airborne insurgents? Maybe see if the shellfish are interested in joining the melee? It's not going to happen, though. Evolution isn't about justice, it's about survival. We live, we breed, we die. If we miss step two and the music stops, then someday we'll end up stuffed and studied in a natural history museum, puzzled over and largely forgotten by snot-nosed children of some other species; sentient, superior and unfamiliar to us.

I swirl the last of my wine. My credit card lies on the table in absence of subtlety. I am starting to grow concerned for Austin. The worst part of my imagination draws one possible fate: He is in back, pouring sodas for a guest, when his manager instructs him to take the garbage out. He walks outside, mind occupied with home and hearth. A bag in each hand, oblivious to danger, he doesn't notice the line of crows gathering atop the telephone pole, the osprey moving in to cut off his escape route or the Peregrine falcon circling overhead, homing in on his position, ready to draw first blood.

## 12

## An Already Interminable Journey

"...what I want and all my days I pine for is to go back to my house and see my day of homecoming. And if some god batters me far out on the wine-blue water, I will endure it, keeping a stubborn spirit inside me, for already I have suffered much and done much hard work on the waves and in the fighting. So let this adventure follow." — Odysseus, *The Odyssey*

"Prepare for our final descent."

Tell me this right now, pilot, just what exactly do you mean by that? Did you mean to specify "final descent as a group," or maybe you are just blithely prophesying a fiery denouement? No one understands the forces at work here. We should all be howling in terror. 30,000 feet above the Earth and this Boeing 737 is pregnant with 75,000 lbs of steel, blue toilet water and corn-fed all American ass-fat, nothing but three sets of rubber tires to buffer the awkwardness.

Memories flicker, gurgling to the surface as the moment of impact approaches. I scan urgently, desperate to relive a moment—any moment—that isn't this one. All the while, the woman next to me is thumbing casually through her *SkyMall*.

Visions play out in the split screen of my mind's eye, countless scenarios in which we all perish violently, vaporized into ash and painted onto twisted steel. What if the landing gear doesn't go down when it's supposed to go down while instruments in the cockpit say that it is in fact down but it's not? Would the pilot have any way of knowing? Maybe one of the tires has a slow leak. That used to happen to my Chevy Malibu all the time. I would take it to the gas station, fill the front left tire to 44 PSI, and two hours later the steering wheel would start to wobble violently when I drove above 50 MPH. What if that happened to us? What would be our recourse? We can't call time out, take a knee and rest on a cloud while taking turns blowing into the valve stem, and this lunatic lady is window-shopping themed throw pillows purposely shaped and colored as to mimic buttermilk pancakes.

All fear abates at touchdown. Wheels and Earth reunite as needle to vinyl, scratching the score to the end credits of my vacation. Twenty-four hours ago I was driving through Sonoma; now I'm back in frozen New York's corporate purgatory. I never really left it, as Time Off is Time On to the corporate masters. The reward for six months of toil is 5.86 paid vacation days. I took 14 off, trading caution for wind. Now money is thin. I'll be using breakfast tips to pay travel expenses put on my credit card. The lady next to me is fingering the trigger on her Visa over some plush waffles and I'm cutting the budget on actual food.

Deplaning is excruciating. We're packed in here like Pez. No exit until the candy tab in queue before us discharges. Most of us understand the ritual at this point—grab your bag and go—but there's always one party that can't coalesce with the urgency of the pack. This time it's a mother of three, scramble-headed and overwhelmed by her own spawn. I feel a pang of sympathy for her. Not for her struggles with the kids per se—she dug those holes—but rather for the deluge of judgment she now has to endure. One hundred eyes on 50 craned necks bore into her, trying to will her into motion. These people need to relax, shelve their contempt and lend a little sympathy to her priorities, foreign as they may seem. I've learned to mitigate my own anxiety in these moments. If ever there were a situation outside of my control, it's waiting to exit an aircraft. This lady has a flock to herd and between three and five carry-ons to untangle before she can clear the path. At that point, and not before, the rest of us will be on our way home. We'll remove our shifted-during-flight bags from the overhead compartments, cruise past the Cinnabons and the Hudson Newses in the terminal, collect our checked luggage and catch our cabs and our buses to go home to our better halves, as well as the toilets where we celebrate most of our shits.

I'm only anxious to get home out of habit. Nothing there to look forward to. I fantasize about this woman never budging, never getting her shit together. In my dream she has an infinite amount of children, and her row is a clown car with a stream of preadolescents scooting off their seats and tugging at her sweater for attention. Her overhead compartment is endless bags; as she fusses one down into the aisle another appears in its place. Stall, lady, stall. Maybe if she lingers long enough, the pilot and passengers will reach a consensus: we never should have left California. It's 80 degrees at LAX with no wind. My toes belong in sand. I should be splayed beneath a palm tree, not hoarding all the steely reserve I can to endure life in New York. Come on, people, let's turn this around.

Unfortunately I underestimated this woman. She's less mess than ninja. The best efforts of her unruly, rambunctious children are suddenly thwarted with surgical precision. A few moments of visible anxiety vanish as she finds her feet, wielding discipline and love as sword and shield. Her young—well-versed in the rules— recognize her authority the moment she channels her voice, filing behind her with military efficiency. Damn. Baggage claim will be a hustle, then I have four trains to ride. The third train is the shortest leg; the 1/2/3 from Penn Station to Times Square. Between the wait and the one-stop ride, it's only slightly faster than exiting the station and crossing the distance on foot. Upon arrival the train is packed to capacity, but I don't believe in capacity. I shove on, my Gregory Internal Frame Hiking Pack swallowing the square footage. The door snaps shut less than an inch behind me. Every eye is on me, drawing the collective ire of a suddenly unified flock of strangers. Everyone wants to glare at the biggest asshole on the train. I don't care. In only one stop their rage will disperse harmlessly as I melt back into the warm embrace of anonymity.

The train arrives at Times Square, doors opening on the right. I shoulder my pack to depart through the opposite side...but am stopped by an invisible resistance from behind. Something—or someone—is holding one of the straps. Who in the shit? I'll kill him! I look back for the culprit, bracing for fisticuffs. My aggressor is karmic, not sapien. My strap is caught in the doors, and the train rolls onward with me in it. I won't be leaving until we reach a stop where the doors again open on the left. It's a 45-minute side quest to Harlem added to an already interminable journey.

Home groans reluctantly into view. I cut through the park towards my apartment, walking slower the closer I get. This feels all wrong. My doorknob is cold, the latch unwelcoming to my keys. The stairs seems steeper, air stale and foreboding. My bedroom opens under duress. I flip the light switch on and right back off. My bag slides to the floor with a reluctant thud. I've been gone for two weeks, a luxurious vacation in the corporate world, but I do not feel refreshed. I don't feel right at all. Two weeks is an *amuse-bouche*, only the fleeting bouquet of adventure, and now I'm ravenous. If I go back to work I will return instantly, dangerously close to my breaking point. I know this feeling too well. The hotel is understaffed as it is. My absence was tolerated, not embraced. And I have to make that money back.

Routine returns easily enough as I retrace the footsteps I know by heart until it becomes automatic. Sandwich from the deli, a movie via HBO On Demand and three Yuenglings. My to-do list vanishes as my beard is shaved, teeth brushed, alarm set for 4 a.m. As much as ever, I am fully reengaged into New York life. I lie in bed, waiting for sleep to take me, gazing around the room with a smile. There, perched against the door next to my boots sits my bag, fully packed.

## 13

## Kangaroo Court of Fighting Fish

We are the soldiers of sustenance, well-versed in our individual roles and unified by a blanket sense of urgency. The in-room dining telephones are dueling for attention, the soundtrack for the apex of the morning. There's at least an hour left of hard fighting before any kind of letup. The line cooks are fully engaged with egg and flame, breaking yolks into vegetable oil and sizzling bacon on a massive griddle. Stewards shuffle around the back, pulverizing oranges and grapefruits into fresh juice. The expeditor is furiously wiping fingerprints off the perimeter of plated eggs benedicts and bowls of steel-cut oatmeal. I'm working the bread station, a blur of popping toast and flashing blades. In one moment I lead the fray, barking commands and stuffing croissants into folded linen. In the next, I am dragged off the floor for a word with Chef.

This office is devilishly comfortable, the luxury box of an abattoir. Two cozy armchairs face a heightened desk cluttered with paperwork in various stages of being processed and ignored. Two glass vessels sit adjacent to each other, each home to brilliantly colored betta fish. Also known as Siamese fighting fish, these creatures look like tropical orchids and behave like starved pitbulls. If dropped into a shared container they will instantly attack each other, relenting only when one is mortally wounded and swimming sideways to the surface in defeat. Somehow this captivity is worse; a bizarre purgatory. There in plain view, your mortal enemy, starkly apparent but separated by an invincible pane of glass. Life is a constant state of tension, ever in fear of death at the hands of your opponent, ever enraged by his presence, naught to do but swim laps.

This is the HR director's office. In the corporate universe, the humanity of the staff is always on trial, never more so in the kangaroo court of human resources. No need for a trial in this case. I'm guilty, having been self-sabotaging my position here for months. I can't stand my supervisor, and I'm not at all quiet about it. She was promoted for the worst kind of reasons: smiling strategically and supplicating to our masters whenever they roll into the kitchen. She's a corporate darling, never complaining about anything real, lending input only to address cosmetic, symptomatic issues. Regarding the philosophical and structural malignancies of our department, she is either willfully ignorant or exceptionally blind to reality. Never mind she doesn't know shit about food and is incapable of delegating any task. Never mind her club-footed managerial style. Never mind the questions she "axes." Never mind her fitful relationship with the differences between "their," "there," "they're," "your," "you're," et cetera. Never mind her chemical addiction to wrongness; she knows when to kneel, so by all means empower her over her talented, intelligent peers with their dangerous notions of free will and self-awareness.

I'm definitely out of strikes here. Third time in HR, same problem as the last time, which itself was awfully similar to the time before that. My neck is well-acquainted with the chopping block at this point. The Chef-ecutioner sits to my right, the director throned behind the fish. It's an emotional exchange. Both of these characters have fought for me in the past, trying to help me fit in. Agony is, they know how good of a job I do. How much skin I lay down every day. I wish I could meet their expectations, just lower my shoulders and shut the fuck up enough to keep my job. I carry the staff most days, but my temper has recently worn down to the nub, metal grinding on metal. Managers from other departments overheard me swearing. My mind is everywhere but work, and I carry it on my face. I've been done here for a while. Selling $14 bowls of Raisin Bran to grouchy millionaires doesn't satisfy the innermost desires of my heart. I'm challenged but not stimulated. Every morning is the same puzzle: How to be proactive; how to motivate the cooks; how to shuttle food up in a timely, accurate fashion; how to give a shit. Mining for meaning is the biggest challenge. I'm swimming around in this bowl, bumping against the glass, and all I want to do is fight.

The chef is worked up, but he's wasting his time. I think he thinks I might try to save my job. The HR director is listening, responding, echoing his concerns, amplifying the depth of my transgressions, broadcasting in plain language how awful they think I am. This is so boring. I want to tell them the truth, that I know all this. I know what attitude you want me to have: You want me to be a good little pet, to shut up and swim quietly. Can't do it. Can't fake it. So I'm suspended, pending investigation. Only one choice left, really. Do I want to be fired or quit? There are certainly benefits to being fired. (Unemployment, baby!) And if that's what I want, I can easily bypass all that suspension shit right here. I could tell the truth for 30 seconds. That would be enough to get the boot right this moment. Or maybe I could tell them to go fuck themselves. It's a barbaric thing to do, but it feels somehow appropriate anyway. The darker side of me yearns for such a release. Wouldn't it be nice to get paid for doing nothing for six months? I could play *Lego Harry Potter* on Xbox and catch up on *Glee*. They don't want that; I can see it on their faces. How expensive is it to get rid of James? Yeah, he's a problem, but God is money, so let's weigh our options.

It's ultimately a spiritual question. I read something brilliant recently in *The Art of Fielding* by a rookie novelist named Chad Harbach. Through the lips of his character Owen he says,

"A soul isn't something a person is born with but something that must be built, by effort and error, study and love." Getting myself fired here is the same as writing myself a dozen checks. One sideways word to manipulate the tempers in this room and I get to skate free for half a trip around the sun. Let the government buy *me* some steel-cut oatmeal for a while. Nothing is really free, though. Every decision has a cost, and in this case the price tag has a portion of my soul etched into the barcode. No sale.

So I resign, eschewing the ignoble luxury of unemployment checks. Keep your money, government. Use it to pay a fireman or something. I'll hang on to my soul for now, for ever, and if you ever need help finding yours, I'm on Facebook.

## 14

## Joss Whedon's Seventh Avenger

We went to see *The Avengers* on opening day, buying Fandango tickets the morning of and arriving at the theater well ahead of time. I had been looking forward to this for a long time, and I'd be shot in the back before I settled on substandard seating for a film of this scale. I had to see these inimitable heroes on screen. I consider myself one of them.

No, really. *The Avengers* cast used my former hotel of employ as their official headquarters for the Manhattan film shoot, and I delivered their room service on a daily basis. I was the seventh Avenger, serving coffee, delivering the newspaper, providing a bounding start to the day so the rest of the team could save it. I'm partially full of shit, but they really did stay with us. Chris Evans was nothing like his avatar, eschewing old-school wholesome principles in favor of absurdly expensive alcohol. Likewise, Tom Hiddleston was hardly the blackhearted god of mischief he plays on screen. Friendly, polite and talkative, he was a delight. Every morning for him began with a grotesquely healthy smoothie made from pulverized romaine lettuce and green apples. The only thing disconcerting about him was his inability to answer the door wearing anything more than a towel. Fool me once, Loki, just once. Shame on you.

Then there was Joss Whedon, the real superhero of the team...with real superhero problems. Quiet and solemn, never smiling but not impolite, the director needed coffee the most. I can't imagine the emotional weight this man carried throughout the production process. The scope and ambition of pulling off *The Avengers* film is rivaled only in human history by the Three Gorges Dam spanning the Yangtze River. His tasks? Flesh out six hero characters and one villain, pay homage to 72 years of comic-book history, satiate a rabid fan base, establish an interesting and believable conflict, choreograph a large-scale urban-battle sequence and balance half a dozen actors with bloated egos playing half a dozen superheroes with bloated egos. Have at it, Tex.

We got great seats. I bought some Peanut M&M's and Julie dragooned the cashier into selling her some Twizzlers: "Listen, shithead. Don't tell me you are out of Twizzlers; there's a pack left in the display case, now crack it open and give me what I want!" Real heroes.

They exist, you know. Remember this past May Day? Seattle? A hundred idiots, dressed in black hoodies and balaclavas, attacked the downtown American Apparel. Armed with wooden staves, they really did a number on the storefront. These were not heroes. They were a flash mob of unruly cowards, throwing a very public temper tantrum with no discernible motive or message. I don't know; maybe I don't get the point of anarchy, or maybe I don't accept that the point of anarchy is that there is no point. It's like an episode of *Cops* where I'd actually root for the cops. If I had still lived there, it would have been tempting to go downtown and crack some heads.

I wasn't alone. Enter Phoenix Jones, real-life resident superhero of Seattle. You can see him in action on YouTube, wearing a wetsuit and confronting rowdy bar-hoppers with a can of pepper spray. On May Day, when the street rats attacked the mall, Phoenix answered the call no one made. He put on his rubber outfit, grabbed his pepper spray, went downtown and began dispersing dissidents. I think he's a complete moron, but I kind of wished I was there with him. Man, do I hate street rats. Insane body odor, ungainly backpacks, forehead tattoos, aggressively begging for leftovers, and for no decent reason, they always have a dog. Why? If it's so hard to feed yourself, why do you own a pet? I applaud you, Phoenix. Stand your ground and execute the mission. I've got your back, but pepper spray ain't my style. I'm more of a fungo-bat-and-trash-can-lid kind of a guy, if that's cool.

They attacked American Apparel? That's the target of a collective rage? Group-think a little harder next time, dumbasses. American Apparel is arguably lame, sure, but much worse villains remain out there. How about the Koch brothers? Those billionaire Tea-Party founders, the puppeteers who galvanize the crazy half of the crazy party to sabotage health care and humiliate gay people. Go smash up their storefront. I'll help!

Avengers was awesome. I don't know how to review films; just trust me, it was fantastic. It was bananas. I'm embarrassed by how much I liked this film, how by the end of it my face actually hurt from smiling for so long. The audience seemed to like it, too. I counted at least a half dozen applause breaks. I kept reading that the movie shattered box-office records worldwide. It seems we have a superinfatuation in this country, as well as globally. It's not slowing down, either. There's another *Batman* in the pipe, and another *Spider-Man*. *Superman* is due for a reboot, and on and on. We have a hero addiction.

Perhaps we crave heroes because the ones we thought we had keep failing. Tiger Woods is a slut, so is Eliot Spitzer. Mark McGwire took steroids. Chris Brown beat the shit out of Rihanna. Paterno, Bellichek, and on and on. The dominoes keep falling. John Edwards, the adulterous, two-faced snake-oil salesman, running for president on his "Two Americas" meme, oblivious to the grotesque, duplicitous irony of his own goddamn message, killing his wife who was already dying on her own. Leveraging earnest campaign donations to paper over a damp stain.

It's such a bummer, this unsubtle trend.
Does anyone ever not fly too close to the sun?
CNN breaking news: Your wings are made of wax.
So what is left? What is the last vestige of
heroism? We know what it's supposed to be, the
trope is well-traveled. Don't justify your means
with ends, tell the truth, stay humble, rescue
damsels, recycle, eat local, be a gentle and
empathetic lover, avoid red meat, watch *The
View*, take a vow of poverty. You don't need a
sidekick, or a cave, or a utility belt, or a cape, or
Black Widow's erupting bustline. Just shut the
fuck up and "Walk the Line," quoth my favorite
raven, Johnny Cash. Keep your eyes wide open all
the time and walk the line, like nobody does.
Heroism is merely a vision, unsteady and
untenable, a platonic ideal, no more than a
dreamscape. It exists only in the theater of the
mind, with an infinite running time, all ages, $0
on the widest screen that never existed, played in
all four dimensions. Please silence your cell
phones.

## 15

## Apex Predator > Breakfast Bitch

I stalk my prey downwind and uphill, crouched, muscles taut. A real predator is never anxious nor hurried, not even at full sprint. I lay silent in the reeds, waiting for my quarry to err. That's when I strike. I'm a hunter. Job Hunter.

Craigslist is jungle, and I am panther. Set your own conditions, maintain the high ground, yield nothing, stay silent, tread on roots and mossy spots and keep low to the soil. Know what to click, what to avoid. Think like my victims, learn their movements. This is my true occupation. My resume reads "Service Industry Professional," but I specialize in job acquisition. My next kill will be Number 15 since moving to New York City, bringing the lifetime count to 32. I treat jobs like carcasses, stripping them of hide and meat until it's time to eat again. The last catch was a big one, akin to a moose or an elk. I was able to feed for over a year, a veritable eternity. I try to use the whole buffalo, but I'm no Apache. If the taste is wrong, I'll leave it for hungrier dogs.

Beware the open call: a time window of 2 p.m. to 4 p.m. to line up, get interviewed, weighed and measured. That's not my turf. I'm a bald, white male with a bald, white problem. No way to stand out. Open calls are the realm of gorgeous actresses with flat stomachs. I have an edge in experience, and my cover letter is an elegant, layered masterpiece of near-classic literature. It's the visual that kills me. Broad shoulders and a square jaw lose to fuck-me heels and an artful neckline every time.

*If interested, please email cover letter and resume to unstimulatingfoodandbeveragegig@job. craigslist.org. Paste resume directly into body of document. Emails with attachments will be ignored.*

And then those two magic words: Cover Letter. My quiver is full of deadly-accurate self-descriptors, active verbs and relevant examples of my intestinal fortitude and demonstrable excellence. I will be hired. This is not a discussion, there will be no floor debate, we shall bypass the court of appeals and sign this directly into law. I start on Monday, and I need to bring six pens, a pair of black dress pants, shoes that can take a shine and a cash bank of $100. Questions?

I wait. I don't chase game; it comes to me. I possess the luxury of choice. Something with benefits that pays well, is close to my cave, or at least a straight shot on the N. Apex predators don't change trains. Also, I won't shave my beard again. It was an act of deference the first time. Utter submission. I kneeled.

Two or three weeks have passed, a welcome break from the insane grind of being everyone's breakfast bitch. I scan the vista for my mark, spear sharpened, lurking in shadow, verging on a pounce, prescient of this exhausted metaphor and its desperate scramble to survive the paragraph. Ultimately the job hunt is a numbers game. Strategy, tactics, animal instinct; they can help. The routine calls for diligence. Stalk the internet and fling some well-worded crap into the ether. Maybe some will stick and I'll get a callback.

I'll have to wait tables; it's what I do now. I didn't go to college for it—no one does—but it's a paper chase, and not a bad one. I have to eat so I'll keep at it, but I soon must look farther afield. Hunt something that hunts back. I long for that old fear. True satisfaction is the product of struggle and conquest, and I'm ready for bigger game.

## 16

## When I'm Dead, Don't Touch My Shit

My resume reads like the list of ingredients in a pack of cigarettes. Most of the components are toxic or poisonous, many completely unrecognizable, and none seem to go together in any kind of purposeful way. "Acetone, naphtelene, cadmium, ammoniac, and it says here that you studied Classical Civilization at Boston University? Can you explain that choice?" All potential employers can decipher from my resume is that none of it is good. I must have more in common with cigarettes after all, because people keep smoking me anyway. Fortunately I can still get into bars.

I'm simultaneously trying to help a friend find a job in Los Angeles. In the midst of my own search, he's sending me his resume. It's not a burden, but a welcome respite. I could use a break from my own grind: the grueling repetition of scanning Craigslist, composing a cover letter, pasting a resume into the email, scheduling an interview, riding a train to said interview, etc. It's interminable. And then, after all that drudgery, they have the gall to ask, "When can you *start* working?"

I would rather help with someone else's resume than tinker with my own. Hell, I'd rather write my own epitaph.

Here Lies Parky

1980-2014

Wingspan 6'2"

"When I'm dead, don't touch my shit."

Some people have terrific resumes, mouth-watering menus of how impossibly wonderful they are. It details where they went to school, what they studied, and how serendipitously relevant every second of their existence thus far is to the job they are applying for. One can look over their work history and witness growth from every position, that their career path curls ever upwards towards a beautiful crescendo of professional determinism. Isn't life a peach?

I scrawl my resume with a black paintbrush. Something short of pride shadows every line. Yes, I live in the "garden studio" apartment. That means "basement." Andy the Android still answers to a Seattle phone number. My email is a free Gmail account. I went to an expensive school and earned a worthless degree. I helped John Kerry lose to the worst president in history. I sold zoo memberships, waited tables at a million restaurants and used to manage Farmers Markets. Every stop was the same. Thrilling at first, the new backdrop was stimulating; it was an adventure. Learning the system, memorizing my responsibilities, getting to know the team. That I could always do. It was the maintenance, handling the crushing boredom that comes with serving as a cog in someone else's machine. That's the impossible nightmare: wrapping a tie around my neck every morning, cinching the knot, shackling myself to my master's illusions.

I desperately want to write a truthful resume.

**Parky**
**400 sq. ft. apartment**
**Un-hip neighborhood**
**New York, NY 11102**

Education

BA in Classical Civilization completed with lowest possible GPA

Goal

Hard-boiled, travel-weary misanthrope looking to fool employer long enough to be eligible for maximum unemployment benefits.

Relevant Experience

**Breakfast Bitch, Uppity Hotel for Millionaires. 2012ish**

- Begrudgingly delivered breakfast on a rolling cart for some reason

- Tolerated idiotic supervisor until mortally incapable of doing so

- Unjustly forced to shave magnificent beard to participate in grotesque facade

**Window Dude, Woodland Park Zoo. 2005**

 - Lovelessly sold admission to families wishing to observe incarcerated slave-beasts

 - Mastered level 50 on free online game Desktop Tower Defense

 - Sadly ate lunch whilst staring and empathizing with self-loathing clan of tapirs

**Campaign Fundraiser, Democratic National Committee. 2004**

- Raised funds for inferior political minds of John Kerry and the execrable John Edwards

- Failed to terminate the dangerously incompetent presidency of Bush Jr.

- Tried to fuck Director of Street Canvassing

References:

Julie Sholt, Ex-girlfriend. Ask her what I did to deserve this.

555-1657

Marvin Blotchski, Alcoholic Assistant Manager, McDivey's Dive Bar. Call between 4 and 4:30 p.m.

555-0898

Enrique Sanchez, Parole Officer. Help me get him off my back.

555-1221

Truth-tellers don't get hired. Not by restaurants, unless they want to be a suit. No waiter is ever just a waiter. We're all desperately dreaming of a better life as we refill water glasses and frenetically cocoon silver within linen. I know I do. I pace from kitchen to dining floor to dish pit and back, scribbling ideas on a pad of paper I keep in my back pocket at all times, trying to spit-shine my vitriol just enough to make it marketable. I'm not working with much. Sometimes I think I have ability; sometimes I think I'm just a fantastically eloquent whiner. What I'm working with is shit. Black, viscous shit, albeit nitrogen-rich. The best kind of fertilizer I've got for now, since I'm not yet a corpse.

## 17

## How Much of an Asshole We are
## Being Right Now

I'm moving in with the first man who ever kissed me.

Apartment-hunting here is a ghastly experience. The realtors are especially sharky, charging a huge cut and human-trafficking you from dump to dump until you give up and sign something, anything. Few details matter in the NYC apartment hunt. I can count a definitive two: Is it cheap? Are there bed bugs? If the answer is yes, followed by no, then it's a miracle.

Three months ago my current roommate asked me to take a permanent hike on account of he wants his girlfriend to move in. I countered that perhaps he should be the one to leave, maybe join an Alaskan fishing company or take up migrant farming. Alas, my size advantage and intellectual superiority are trumped every time by his lease rights. If ever there was an event that would precipitate me giving up on New York City, this was it. I was fully resigned to going back to Seattle, all beat up and defeated, no throne, no belt of scalps, no trophy to brandish for the locals. Instead we all bought a giant fake fish.

The first warm day of spring happened to fall on Donnelly's birthday, and we were throwing him a party. Donnelly is the kind of guy who buys all the crap he needs and wants for himself anyway, so if you get him a present, it has to be outside the box, carved out of wood, shaped like a swordfish, and mounted above the flatscreen. The trouble with purchasing a gag gift is trying to hide your disdain for the saleswoman who holds sincere feelings of sentimentality and appreciation for the tacky monstrosity in her possession. We were a large pack of 30-something artists, half drunk from brunch, piling $10 bills on the counter and asking, "How much for the tuna?"

The woman's wounded face betrayed her— she knew the fate of her pet. Nemo or Wanda or whatever this beast's name was, he wasn't going to a loving home or a kitschy seafood restaurant where he belonged. He was going to serve his time in hell as a fantastical symbol of glorious hipster irony. Imagine the conversation piece he would become.

"Nice fish."

"Hey, thanks!"

"Goddamn, you are interesting."

"Yes, I am."

The party was fantastic. Strange Greek sausages grilled slowly over the coals. Someone passed around a bag of ribs-flavored potato chips. There was beer and margaritas, and salad for no reason, and a man mowing the grass behind the adjacent apartment building. The birthday boy, prescient of the mortality of my residence, turned to me and asked, "Hey man, know why that guy is cutting the lawn? He's about to rent out the apartment behind all that grass. You should go live there."

I grabbed Bruner, and we checked it out. It was perfect. Absolutely perfect. Very clean, definitely no bugs, brand-new bathroom and kitchen, lots of lighting, and a sure-as-shit back yard. In a city choked with concrete, we would have our own patch of grass. We could start a garden, co-parent some peonies, install an above-ground plastic kiddie pool, forge a future within the fiery womb of cohabitation.

Bruner is a good dude, fiercely loyal, sensitive and passionate. He's no coward. Bruner steps up and does the right thing for a friend in need. Two or three months prior, I was having a bad day. Cratering, I trudged to the local watering hole. They call it Sparrow Tavern, but we call it The Bird. I was chasing good beer after bad, exacerbating my mood with liquid depressant. Worse yet, I got the hiccups. Aside from being socially annoying, for me hiccups have the tendency to precede projectile vomit. I needed a cure, ASAP.

The Sparrow bartender is a bit of a witch doctor. An ace mixologist, Mr. Freeland has a tender manner with even the most brutish of customers, and multi-tasking comes as naturally to him as breathing or digestion. "Parky, I have the solution. But it will only work one time, and I can't give it to you." I told him the fuck he couldn't. He shook his head and kept drying the glass in his hand. My hiccups persisted, and so did I.

"Fuck you, Free; fix what ails me, you son of a bitch!" Free's cold eyes read, "*Mentula conatur Pipleium scandere montem*, another mortal found my doorbell." He leaned across the wood top and whispered to Bruner, who laughed. "What is going *hiccup* on?" I shouted. "What are you two *hic* talking about?" Bruner shook his head. Denied. Consensus was taken, and I was left to suffer. I sat in a rage, grinding my teeth, tearing my beverage napkin, hiccupping miserably on my stool, looking for faces to punch, choking back tears and vomit. I was in physical pain; why wouldn't anybody help me? "Cure me, you assholes!"

"All right, Parky. I'll cure you." Bruner downed his whiskey, pushed off from the bar, and stepped brazenly into my personal space. When I opened my mouth to protest he kissed me full on, hard as he could. The old element-of-surprise trick. I tried to pull away, but his hands were clamped around the back of my skull in the unrelenting vice grip of tough love. Resistance was both futile and unnecessary, so I squeezed my eyes shut and took my medicine like an adult. Though his tongue stayed in his own mouth, his beard scraped against mine. The kiss lasted maybe fifteen seconds, but it left a permanent mark. And my hiccups were gone, without a trace, perhaps forever.

It felt something a bit shy of disgusting. Bruner is fairly pretty for a man, but he has facial hair and big hands and he smells like a car fire. There's not much there that I find sexually relevant, but it didn't feel especially wrong or evil. Supposedly this sort of thing is an abomination in the eyes of God. You'd think there would have erupted a jet of Hellfire, or a screaming demon to contend with, at the very least an bouquet of sulphur steaming up from the cracks in the floor.

Leviticus 20:13 – *"If a man lie with mankind, as he lieth with a woman, both of them have committed an abomination: they shall surely be put to death; their blood shall be upon them."*

Bring it, bitch. This Levi was the craziest of 40 dead-guy co-authors of the Bible and the only one getting specific about this, channeling the will of God into a statement of eternal bigotry.

Are you sure you heard him right? This is important. It affects the species: If you are right, we've got a lot of undoing to get done. First off, it's gallows for Ellen, Elton, at least one of those Jonas virgins, and we have to make sure the ghost of Dumbledore is writhing in a lake of magma. If you are wrong, well, we've got a problem, because an awful lot of gay folks and their friends out there would prefer they be treated like human beings with dignity and respect.

We can start by letting them get married. I understand a plurality of North Carolinians don't think I should marry Bruner. I'm with them; I don't want to marry him either. Someday I'll marry a pretty girl with soft skin and weak ankles, but it pisses me off that a bunch of hick voters say I can't. I'm so sick of this homophobic group-think shit. What's the fucking problem, exactly? Gay marriage isn't something that happens to you, it's something that happens for someone else. It's entirely avoidable if you don't want it. "The Bible says it's bad!" parrot thousands who never muscled up to read so much as *The New York Post*. Yet anti-gay references in the Bible are vague and rare, and none fall under the Commandments category: the only clear list of Dos and Don'ts in the thing.

The trouble with using an ancient text transcribed and translated several dozen times over is that you end up with an even gayer orgy of scrambled-up ideas and irrelevant, contradictory bullshit that doesn't work for most folks. If we write every passage in Leviticus into law, there would be no bacon cheeseburgers, or cheeseburgers at all for that matter—ain't kosher—and it would be perfectly acceptable and vigorously encouraged to trade and own human beings. The Bible has a lot of pretty passages about how the Earth came to be, and who begat whom back in the day, and there are a couple "Love thine enemy" passages that ought to be followed by all of us, but as a comprehensive Existence Rulebook, it's a lousy piece of shit.

What an inglorious mess, all of these registered voters cherry-picking a passage from the Bible as the leveraging agent for their knee-jerk reaction to man-on-man matrimony. It doesn't make one damn bit of sense. If you hate The Gays, you'd better hate The Cheeseburgers, because there's way more Biblical God-speak about keeping milk off meat than there is about keeping man-meat off man-meat.

Our aggregate decisions matter, despite what The Good Book says or doesn't say. In 1883 a perfectly human black dude was trying to play professional baseball—he was a catcher named Moses—and some dingleberry asshole named Cap Anson yelled, "Get that nigger off the field!" and other such crap until we made a national mistake for the next 70 years: boring, uninspired baseball played solely by white people. Can you imagine? Now let's all sit down, talk to each other like adults, and consider learning from our mistakes before history soon tells us how much of an asshole we were being right now.

So we got the apartment. It's been a weird week. I got dumped—by a woman—and the weather report calls for warm temperatures with 100% chance of calamitous change. I somehow have to fill half of an apartment. There's a furniture void; we fall far short of even Spartan-status living. Priority number one is going to be the yard. We need outdoor seats, some kind of flooring to stave off the mud, citronella candles,

oil lanterns and a grill. The yard—our garden—
shall be the newest iteration of Rome, the capital
rotunda at the epicenter of Western thought. This
is our olive tree, where we'll cross our own
Rubicon and declare yet another list of
mandatory amendments to the Self-Evident
Rights of All Mankind. Once we've done that and
propped up half a dozen tiki torches, *then* we'll
get around to calling the electric company and
throwing down a rug or two.

## 18

## The Devil I Know, the Demon I'll Become

Like one of those *Gone Wild* Girls, I took my shirt off in the bar to a cacophony of popping flashbulbs. "Okay James, suck in your gut and make a six pack." I clenched my abdomen to no effect. Sal might as well have asked me to bank a chicken wing off the international space station and land it in Africa. "Now blast your stomach out as far as it can go." I did as instructed, taking care not to knock over anyone's cocktail. Sal strung a tape measure around the mass grave of deli sandwiches, domestic beer and Chips Ahoy that comprise my midsection and recorded his findings.

Memorial Day, my last 24 hours of willfully negligent consumption. I spent it bloating up as much as possible. Breakfast was a bacon-egg-and-cheese and a carton of orange juice. A turkey club and a bag of salt-and-vinegar potato chips served as lunch. For dinner: a slice of buffalo-chicken pizza smothered in bleu cheese.

Sodium, carbohydrates, dairy; the more the better. I had to get weighed in, and turning my liver into foie gras ensured I'd look as awful as possible. Swallowing six or seven Pabsts completed the final push.

Sal is the brainpower behind the Second Annual Great Astoria Gut-Off. Twenty dudes, $100 buy-in, six pack of abs by Labor Day. Winner take all, because there can be only One out of this slovenly pack of fat Highlanders. Sal is enigmatic, a double agent of wellness and self-destruction. He's a regular drinking buddy, a close friend to saturated fat and fermented malt, and an enthusiastic proponent of metabolic exercise. Now he's the founder and moderator of a summer-long fitness competition.

I don't plan to win. There's no way to game the system; it's not a measurement of weight loss, BMI, waist size or anything else quantifiable. On the national Day of Labor we'll simply bare our chests, flex and subject ourselves to the judgment of the masses. Our fate lies in the hands of The People. This is the male equivalent of a wet t-shirt contest, minus any element of actual attractiveness. I didn't join for the money, but for

105

the motivation. I crave the carrot dangling from the end of the stick. The only way out of the swamp I'm in is to start moving, and I desperately need an inspirational spectre to give myself a jump.

The job hunt has gone a bit cold. I'm starting to suspect foul play, that some names on my reference list have soured and turned their backs on me. I had three promising interviews last week, dolling myself up for the occasion in name-brand male elegance. Dark olive Banana Republic chinos, Ben Sherman Albini button-down, sharp Steve Madden Brakker sneaks: chic, form-fitting, hard-hitting. I'd hire me. Yet every time I check my phone, Andy the Android has nothing to report other than the latest desperate email from Nancy Pelosi panhandling for money.

The hottest lead I received was for a room-service phone job at the Trump International Hotel. More eggs. It's a "The devil you know..." kind of situation. Yes, I hate schlepping breakfast, but at least I can do it with confidence. Dossier of resumes and references tucked under my arm, I marched into the lobby. Working the dais were three Charlie's Angels, perfect 10's with high dagger heels, snake-like pantyhose and viciously sleek albeit conservative dresses. "I'm here for the opening in room service," I bleated at all three of them. The tremor in my voice betrayed my anxiety, but even I didn't know the source. Either I was nervous about the interview, intimidated by the radiant sexuality of these Amazons, or maybe the tsunami warning in my colon was wailing in advance of imminent trouble. "Find a deep toilet, Parky; something with plenty of flow. We've got meat to move down here!"

One of the sex lizards led me outside to the patio to wait for the manager on duty. It was an odd place for an interview considering the weather, nearly 100 degrees with a blanket of humidity. No shade, either, so the sweat beaded up instantly upon my traitorous scalp. She poured me a glass of ice water, which served more for damage control than refreshment. The manager took a life age to materialize, leaving me plenty of time to think.

The weigh-in behind me, it would soon be time to reverse direction. I had the plan sketched. Step one was to clean out the engine. From mouth to anus, I had considerable traffic to alleviate. A caustic bottle of cleansing agents comprised of fresh ginger, turmeric and cayenne pepper chilled pensively in my refrigerator. It was designed to liquify the bowels, irritate the colon walls and squeeze out the contents like toothpaste from a tube.

As I finished dwelling on future shits, the manager appeared in a pantsuit and sat down across from me. "So James, tell me, why did you leave your previous job?" I swallowed hard. This woman had piercing eyes, shark-like posture, an extremely sharp pen and plenty of interrogation experience. I squared my shoulders and assailed her with a fusilade of lies and half-truths. I wanted the job, but how badly?

Apparently pummeling her with charm worked: on the way out she asked me how tall I was. Translation: "I like how tall you are." Unfortunately her final question filled the sky with dark, ominous clouds. "So James, would you object to me asking you to shave every day for this job?" Lightning struck behind my eyes, thunder rumbling deep within. If there's one thing I hate in this world, it's when women ask me to shave. I'm all for gender equality, and I earnestly believe we need to do a better job as a nation of acknowledging the strength, professionalism and courage of women in the workplace. That said, the beard is off limits. I can't grow hair on my head, so I grow it on my face. It's really that simple. It frames the jaw, lends color and definition to my pale complexion, and, oh: It's *my* goddamn face. I can only imagine the chain reaction of vitriol unleashed were I to suggest her hairstyle was ugly and inappropriate. "Sure, no problem!" I chirped. *Yo me llamo* "Doormat." *Ay, dios mio!*

Another interview behind me, another manager snooping around my reference list, scanning my past for sources of concern. The urgency compounded every day. There's nothing to be done about it; no way to skip steps. A six pack of abs can't be cultivated overnight, either. It takes a coordinated effort. Crunches alone won't do. Neither will weight loss. I need to cut carbs, build muscle, sculpt my abdominals and burn fat...as much as possible. Fill the fridge with good, clean fuel: Greek yogurt, almonds, fresh eggs, tomatoes, kale, spinach, chicken breasts, salmon, no sugar at all, no white flour anywhere, plenty of fish oil, multi-vitamins and water.

Endless water, at least a tubful, every hour. Each drop swallowed makes its way out somehow, either through my skin or my urine, spiriting toxins and salt away with it. Then comes the exercise.

Something has to happen here. I'm taking too many steps in that direction—self-transmogrifying with vigor—to not. By training like a demon, I'll become one. Horns and scales, a forked tongue and a wicked physique. A salvo of resumes every day, callbacks after promising interviews, air squats, pull-ups, chin-ups, push-ups, incline push-ups, crunches, planking, four-hour bike rides, interval training on the track, running up stairs, jumping rope, eschewing beer for grain alcohol. This is the hardest part, a full month of gritting through pain and soreness, enduring humiliation at the hands of picky and condescending hiring managers. I'm tearing tissue fiber, ignoring discomfort, investing faith in the hope that under these stubborn layers of tummy and mental fat there is a wall of muscle beginning to form, hardening into a sheer face of solid rock.

## 19

## One Last Swift Kick to the Junk

I enjoy drinking wine. Vino pairs well with food, sometimes even as well as experts claim. I just can't stand talking about what amounts to the worst kind of poetry: "A bouquet of blackberries, tobacco and vanilla, mildly tannic and dry on the tongue, medium-bodied with a hint of stone fruit and a long, peppery flutter that fades into a mellow finish." Lies! I won't be a part of it. Any time I hear someone proselytizing about how their favorite Malbec tastes like a sunset, I choke back hate-vomit and have to stop myself from shouting, "It's grapes! The wine tastes like fermented grapes! Shut up and drink!"

Job hunting was getting pretty desperate. Just me and Andy the Android, putting out feelers and riding the MTA from restaurant to restaurant. Poor Andy didn't get a lot of sleep these days. He kept trying to, shutting off his HUD every 60 seconds when I didn't use him under the pretense of needing to "save his screen." I woke him up regularly, checking email for leads on interviews, surfing Craigslist for openings, playing pirated-Yahtzee timekiller Dice With Buddies. Most of all, I just huddled in his magnificent glow while the shadows crept in from all sides.

Almost every server position I interviewed for wanted me to speak enthusiastically about their glorious wine list. Not going to happen. My first choice would be to get my old job back. I used to serve tables at Downtown BBQ. Solid management, great food, consistent money. It wasn't perfect—it was a restaurant job, after all—but I always knew where I stood, what my role was and whom to approach with a problem. Five shifts a week to cover my hierarchy of human needs, plus the management is well-versed in human decency. The biggest perk was the front-of-house staff. Nearly 40 percent gay and almost entirely composed of actors, it made life a party. We sang at the water station, danced in the dish pit, cracked jokes at the POS. It was like working for a flash mob. I put in my resume over a week ago and I'm still waiting to hear word. They do have a wine list, but trust me, they'd much rather me know my beers than my grapes. That I can handle.

"'What do we have on tap?' you ask. I will answer your question with a question of my own: Where, sir/madam, do you fall on the spectrum of flavor? I need to know, because we've got options. The Brooklyn Sorachi Ace, Founders Red's Rye and especially the Peak Organic IPA are the Murderer's Row of hoppy ales. You want to drink them with ribs or chicken, and don't forget to dial up the hot sauce, because otherwise these beers are just going to stand in the middle of your tongue and hammer-toss the meat straight down your throat. You'll put $60 on your credit card and forget what you ate for dinner. If you're a path-of-least resistance/right-lane type, I can recommend the Blue Point Summer Ale. It's mild, lemony and drama-free. It goes with everything because it's a glass of water with beer coloring, but it's a decent option if you prioritize superficial social pressures and would like to perpetuate the facade that you enjoy drinking beer. I warn you, if you order beers like this on a consistent basis, they will leave you wondering which toilet you flushed your life down when the Grim Reaper pays a visit to your bedside.

"Now, 99% of Mankind has already made their choice, but maybe you are special. If you are bold, understanding that life is more than just a series of comfortable escapes, I have a beer for you. It's as black as a shadow with the consistency of liquid velvet. More of an experience than a beverage, drinking it is going to unlock some suppressed memories and wipe others away forever. It tastes like a carbonated glass of black iced coffee, sweetened with the the syrupy residue of an extended waking nightmare. Its given name is Keegan's Mother's Milk Stout, but I call it the 'The Raven.' I recommend pairing it with the dry-aged strip steak or the Texas beef ribs. But whatever you do, pair it with meat. The gods won't appreciate it if you drink this beer without taking a life. Angering Apollo will summon ill-favored winds."

I loved that job.

We all make mistakes, but I'm a fuck-up star. My wrong turns are downright *inspired*. Subsequently, while few ought to dwell on the past, I sit in it like murky bathwater. The Dalai Lama implores us to mind the moment. The present is starving for content, desperate to see

who we are, what our talent is and what we have
to offer the realm of Now, humming like a juicer
and yawning for the next apple. I know this, and
yet I'm lost in a glaze of self-loathing, casting
thoughts into the fishless depths of my memory,
looking for something worthy to reel in. It's a
false hope. I have to throw everything I catch
back and settle for a sweaty bag of McDonald's on
the way home to my partially furnished, outer-
borough basement apartment.

I'd left Downtown BBQ to ship dresses.
You can always tell it's a mistake to quit because
everyone's faces get scrambled-up and
incredulous, their timbres rising at the end of
their inevitable questions. "Why are you *leaving*?"
they marvel. It gets weirder when you explain,
"I'm going to mail ladies wear now. Goodbye." But
that's what I did. This was apparently the sort of
job you could score with a Classical Civilization
degree. I spent four years reading Aeschylus,
conjugating Ancient Greek verbs and studying
Hoplite warfare so I could stand under fluorescent
light and stuff hot pink chiffon into cardboard
boxes. It's hard to square that with the history in
your head. I'd rather have died fending off

Persians at the Battle of Marathon than standing there printing shipping labels.

It didn't help that I worked for crooks.

New York is full of criminals. You see it everywhere, every day. Little kids snatch purses and vanish into the park. Over-served bar hoppers wake up on the subway car they passed out in to find their pockets gently incised, their wallets and iPhones removed. Gastropubs charge $9 for a beer. Wall Street assholes shout at each other all week, whining about the evils of regulation even as their arms are completely submerged in the cookie jar, chocolate all over their faces. Jealous for a cut, we dress-hawkers similarly ripped off customers.

Imagine you are a 16-year-old girl in Akron, Ohio, navigating rough hormonal seas as your body updates factory-installed puberty apps and calc homework is always due tomorrow. You play field hockey but are a goalie, so you don't run as much as the skinny bitches. You aren't fat—you know that much—but every morning is a struggle against the mirror. You read somewhere that corn syrup is the problem, so you are trying to learn how to choke down Diet Coke instead, but aspartame tastes like diecast metal. Prom is coming. Your choices are a bit narrow, but you have the self-esteem to turn down Evan Stuernagel. Everybody knows he was suspended for jerking off to black porn in the library. Holding out paid off. Jeremy Hampton asked you with a tremor in his voice, and his eyebrow kept twitching like it does. He's not just a date, he's *interested* in you.

Fuck, now you need a dress. Mom hands you the credit card and a "Don't tell your father." You don't need *any* dress; you need something from New York Fucking City. This is *Jeremy*. He has those eyebrows. Your simple Google search finds us, and boom, there it is: Janique JO38, an off-the-shoulder number in Midnight Blue, with petal applique and a hip-hugging skirt, and the whole thing flares out awesomely under the knee. Plus it's going to make your tits pop. So you order it, size 8.

We don't have a size 8 in that dress at this time. We don't tell you, because we don't care about you. You don't matter. You are merely a mark. We don't let simple things like inventory

117

get in the way of a sale. So we call the designer and order a size 6. It's a simple fix, really. When that 6 comes in, we just do a few minor alterations. Snip off that pesky 6 tag and give you, the customer, what you want—a size 8 dress. When it comes hurtling through the mail system, it's a bit more snug than you planned. Maybe it's *too* snug, and you need to scramble for a last-minute replacement. Either way, Jeremy is getting a tightly-wrapped date, and your fragile self-image just took another hit to the solar plexus. Did you gain weight? Are you really a size 10 now? Tears, anxiety, disappointment. Poor girl, you deserved better. You would have crushed that dress. For the sake of your superfluous tears, I picked the busiest possible week and spent it at home.

Now my day job was getting a day job, and I'm staying in New York. That wasn't a foregone conclusion three weeks ago. I had a lot of tabs open in my mental browser, and half of them were websites singing the praises of other, easier places. Somewhere with a pool. Nothing would make me happier than to eschew this crap and live somewhere else for a while. Life isn't about being happy, though. At least, not if you're interesting. For me, joy is a drug with diminishing returns, so I'm looking for something stronger. Living easy won't bring happiness any more than marching a few inches forward in the ankle-deep shit of my current existence will. I came here to slay some demons, and I'm not leaving until my belt is adorned with scaly, horned scalps.

A ray of light finally squirmed through the ever-fog, but at a cost. I almost lost Andy. I was trying to help him out by freeing up space on his hard drive—standard maintenance—when he slipped out of my hands and took a digger into the pavement on the corner of 36th and Fifth. Pangs of guilt and terror raked at my heart as his battery and back plate exploded into the crosswalk with an excruciating twang. Fumbling desperately to piece him together, I reassembled his guts in Midtown traffic, pedicabs and city buses honked angrily at my oblivious indifference to their right-of-way.

I can't lose you now, Andy. Not here; not like this. We've been through so much together and we have miles yet to go, old friend. I flipped Andy over, only to be overwhelmed with despair.

His face, his beautiful touchscreen visage, was shattered into a web of fractured glass. I pressed his Power switch, desperate for signs of life. Nothing. Turn on, Andy! Don't quit, don't die here in the street like a bitch! I pressed it again. Eternity. Come on...come on...come on...

"Whrrrr!" he vibrated, struggling, lighting up and fighting for his life. I kissed his shattered face as he queued up the Menu screen. His desktop loaded Dice with Buddies, Words with Friends, Evernote, Gmail. The internet indicator glowed 4Gs. The battery icon filled up, too - all of it - full power. "Look at you, you crotchety old bastard," I whispered. Nothing could stop Andy. He was a juggernaut.

One final symbol appeared: an email. Andy squealed at its presence as if to say, "Check it now, Parky! Come on! My faceplate is fine! Chicks dig scars; we can worry about that later. It might be something good!" Andy was a stubborn little fucker. His smile glowed through even busted teeth. I've dropped him a thousand times, and yet he carried on, more determined now than ever. He got it. He understood that there is no rainbow, that the journey is the destination. He grasped the terrible importance of the moment, and heeded the past only to remind me of texts sent, phone calls missed, once-precious communications left behind. The reception bars on his brow betrayed his true purpose, his unyielding vigilance and devotion to the divine omnipotence of the here and now. When Andy talked, I listen. My fingertip slid roughly over his broken face, but the image below moved as smoothly as the day I bought him. I found the alert and lit it up. "Hi James, this is Mike Sandberg from Downtown BBQ," the screen read. "Sorry it took us so long to get back to you; it's been pretty busy around here. We'd like to have you stop by tomorrow and talk about coming back to the team. Does 2 p.m. work for you?"

I felt a strange warming sensation from the base of my diaphragm. Subtle at first, it permeated upward along my ribs as ivy to brick, surging into and out of my heart, gaining strength. The heat entered my lungs, something like a cooling steam of eucalyptus billowing upward and out, tickling the corners of my mouth and contorting my face into something not unlike a grin. A small snap, and a dull pulse of pain

121

coursed my jaw. I deigned to smile full and wide, pulling a cheek muscle. I guess it had been a while. Nothing like one last swift kick to the junk from a faltering bout of depression.

I snapped Andy's flip-out keyboard shut, tucking it back under the display. No need to respond right away. Better to let Andy sleep. They'll never respect me if I reply in a desperate rush. Besides, I've got shit to do. Anything truly worth a damn can wait an hour.

# Acknowledgements

I never set out to write a book, so I find myself in the awkward position of having more people to thank than I'll ever be capable of, but I'll take a shot anyway. Thank you mom and dad for catching me when I fall, and for never judging or discouraging me, even when my dreams and mistakes are completely congruent. Thank you Jennifer for being a perfect big sister. I could never have survived New York without you. Still might not.

Thank you Sandro for beta testing my crazy ideas, thank you Dave for urging me to keep my ass in the chair, and thank you Jeff for tolerating me over and over again as I bobbed crazily around from career to career looking for footholds. You are my dearest friends.

Thank you Solomon, Jake, Danielle, Brett, Daniel, James, Hari, Lars, Peter, Joe, Derek, Travis, Kevin, Paul, Kevin, Emmett, Brian, Lizzy, Rory, Mark, Scott, Carl, Ron, Dave, Angela, Geoff, Taylor, Paul, Kate, Seth, Billy, Jesse, Toby, Nicole, Jessica, Nick, Ron, Kermit, Gabriel, Travis, the Beards of Comedy, and countless others for being such a huge part of my life as I tried - and failed - to stand up and be funny. Thank you to Jenn and Tyler for chipping in when I needed you in a pinch.

Thank you to all of the idiots and assholes who shaped my life so grotesquely in New York. You are every bit the sound and the fury I heard so much about. In trying to destroy me, you gave me an endless font of material, and while your awfulness is staggering, your potential for humanity is humbling. The struggle to realize it is worth fighting for.

Special thanks to Bryan who lived all of these adventures by my side, my wingman on the stoop and in the bike lanes. Thank you Andy; may you rest in peace, old friend. Thank you to Julie. I call you my copy editor but you are so much more. I shudder to think what this would have been without you. I knew that I could write, but you showed me it was worth it. I'll be needing you again soon.

And thank you to Koei, whoever you are.